Picking
up the
Pieces

A ROSE GARDNER

BETWEEN THE NUMBERS NOVELLA

THIRTY-TWO AND THIRTY-THREE

Denise Grover Swank

ISBN-13: 978-1500714208
ISBN-10: 1500714208

Cover Design: Complete Pixels and Iona Nicole Photography
Developmental Edit: Angela Polidoro
Copy Edit: Shannon Page

Picking
up the
Pieces

by Denise Grover Swank:

Rose Gardner Mysteries
(Humorous Southern mysteries)
TWENTY-EIGHT AND A HALF WISHES
TWENTY-NINE AND A HALF REASONS
THIRTY AND A HALF EXCUSES
FALLING TO PIECES (novella)
THIRTY-ONE AND A HALF REGRETS
THIRTY-TWO AND A HALF COMPLICATIONS
PICKING UP THE PIECES (novella)
THIRTY-THREE AND A HALF SHENANIGANS

Chosen Series
(Paranormal thriller/Urban fantasy)
CHOSEN
HUNTED
SACRIFICE
REDEMPTION

On the Otherside Series
(Young adult science fiction/romance)
HERE
THERE

The Curse Keepers
(Adult urban fantasy)
THE CURSE KEEPERS
THE CURSE BREAKERS

Off the Subject
(New Adult Contemporary Romance)
AFTER MATH
REDESIGNED
BUSINESS AS USUAL

Chapter One

Rose

I stood in my decimated business staring at Joe, the first man I'd ever loved, and Hilary, the woman he couldn't shake, even when he tried.

"Joe, darling." She glided toward him and put her hand on his chest. "Congratulations are in order. You're going to be a daddy."

I sank into one of the three folding chairs that had been set up in the only part of the shop not covered in debris, forgetting how to breathe. "Oh, crappy doodles."

For once, Violet was silent as she watched the couple in front of us, clearly as shocked as I was. Perhaps she was finally having second thoughts about accepting Joe's money, without my knowledge, to save our business.

Joe's face paled and he looked like he was about to pass out. "*What?*"

Hilary flashed him a dazzling smile, as though she expected him to share in her joy. "We're going to have a baby, Joe."

His eyes widened and he shook his head. "No. That's impossible."

"Don't be dense, Joe. You know how babies are made." She pinned her gaze on me, her eyes hardening. "And we made love enough times on the campaign trail to ensure there were plenty of opportunities for it to happen."

Her glare was clearly a challenge. My face burned, but I refused to look away.

Joe's face turned red too, but when he spoke his voice quavered with anger, not embarrassment. "No, you're on the pill."

She delicately placed her fingertips on her collar bone, her perfectly tweezed eyebrows lifting slightly. "Oh. Did I forget to mention that my doctor took me off the pill three months ago?"

Joe's hands clenched at his side as his jaw tightened. "You're lying."

"I'm not…and I have the doctor's report to prove it." She dug into her cream-colored Prada bag and pulled out a folded piece of paper, which she handed to him.

He jerked it away from her, his hand shaking as he read it.

I knew I should leave. Joe's business no longer concerned me, but I couldn't seem to get out of the chair.

Joe tossed the paper at Hilary, shaking his head. "No. I don't believe you. It wouldn't be hard for you to forge this."

She gracefully caught the floating paper and tucked it back into her purse. "I know it's a bit of a shock." She gave him a sympathetic pout. "We hadn't planned on children for a few more years, but we'll have to speed up our plans a little. We can get married in a few weeks like we'd originally planned during the campaign. Momma hasn't cancelled any of the arrangements yet."

Joe took two steps back from her, the vein on his forehead throbbing as he exploded. "I'm not marrying you!"

"Now, Joe. I realize this is a shock—"

"I'm not marrying you!"

She tilted her head to the side, seemingly unfazed by his violent outburst. "Do you really want our baby to be a bastard?"

"You're not pregnant!"

Her eyes narrowed and the snake I knew her to be slipped through the cracks of her polished exterior as she lifted her chin. "And in the entirety of the twenty-nine years we've known each other, have I *ever* bluffed about something of this magnitude, Joseph Robert Simmons?"

And just like that, the fight slid out of Joe and he gasped. Although he had shared very little with me about his time with Hilary, I took his reaction to mean he believed her.

I felt like I was going to throw up. So, it was true. Hilary was pregnant with Joe's baby. I shouldn't have cared, but I did. Anger washed through me and I wasn't sure who I was angry *with*, Hilary for clearly trapping Joe in this situation or Joe for letting it happen.

Joe's mouth gaped open in shock but nothing came out, then he turned to me, horror in his eyes as he pleaded, "Rose…"

For the past month, I'd told him we were over again and again, until I was blue in the face, but Joe refused to believe it. As evidenced by the look of dismay on his face right now. In addition to all of the other changes it would necessitate in his life, his ex-girlfriend turning up pregnant was throwing a huge curve ball into his master plan to win me back.

I shook my head, my eyes filling with tears, unsure how to respond.

Hilary's lips widened into a sly grin. "I made an ultrasound appointment with a doctor here in Henryetta for this afternoon so you can see our baby and hear its tiny little heartbeat."

His head swung around to her, his face white as the snowflakes that had begun falling outside our ripped-apart nursery. "Heartbeat?"

Her smile turned sweeter. "I know! Isn't it amazing?" Her hand smoothed an imaginary wrinkle on her completely flat abdomen. "Our baby already has a heartbeat."

Joe's eyes widened and he looked like he thought that fact was the furthest possible thing from amazing.

"I knew you'd want to hear it, so I arranged everything, which wasn't easy since it's a holiday weekend and you're living in a hick town." She tilted her head and twisted her mouth into yet another version of a pout. "But see how much I love you?" Her smile brightened. "So all you have to do is show up late this afternoon at Henryetta Family Clinic. Five o'clock." She closed the distance between them and kissed his cheek.

"I'll see you later, Joe." She shot me one last glare before turning and heading for the doorway, carefully picking her way through a minefield of broken ornaments, plastic tree limbs, dirt, and broken pots. Before she stepped outside, she stopped and looked over her shoulder at me. "I just love what you've done with the place, Rose." And with that she left and shut the door behind her.

"That witch!" Violet gasped, watching through the window as Hilary sashayed her way to her shiny white Lexus.

I shared her opinion, but at that moment I was more worried about someone else. I stood, clasping my shaky hands together. "Joe."

His eyes were glassy as they met mine and he looked shell-shocked.

"Are you okay?" It was the stupidest question I could possibly ask, but I was at a loss to come up with something better.

He shook his head and swallowed. "I…"

I moved toward him and wrapped my hand around his wrist, gently tugging him toward the chairs. "Come sit down."

He came willingly enough and sat in one of the chairs, looking like he was going to pass out. I took the one next to his, still holding his arm. I was afraid to let go, as if I might be the only thing holding all the bits and pieces of him together.

Violet shuddered and leaned her arms against the back of the folding chair across from us. "Is she right?"

she asked in a prying tone. "Is she really pregnant with your baby?"

He looked up at her, his mouth opening, but nothing came out.

My anger rose up like a billowing cloud. She was interfering. Again. "You stay out of this, Violet! It's none of your business!"

Her eyes flew wide. "And it's *yours*? Haven't you been telling Joe for weeks that it's over between you? More competition shows up and you suddenly want him back?"

"*More* competition?" But I instantly knew she was talking about herself. Could she actually be serious? I would have confronted her more on the topic, but it didn't seem like the time. "Joe needs a friend right now."

"That's right. He needs a friend." She strutted around the empty chair and sat in it, leaning forward. "I'm here for you, Joe."

I sat up in disbelief.

Joe looked more confused than ever.

Maybe Violet was right. I *had* been pushing him away, so why did I feel this push-pull to stay with him now? What kind of mixed signals was I sending? Perhaps my need to help him was actually hurting him. "I'll go." I realized I was still holding his arm, so I released it and started to stand.

Joe's eyes widened in panic. "No, Rose. Stay. *Please*."

Violet hesitated. "I'm worried about you, Joe. I don't want you to be alone."

Joe took several deep breaths. He was barely straddling the line of control and my sister was about to topple him over.

"Violet, please," I pleaded. "Just go. I'll stay with him."

"Well, we still have to discuss the business. There are a lot of things for us to go over."

"Yeah…" Joe lifted his free hand and rubbed his head. "Yeah, she's right."

My back stiffened. I suspected I had a heap more to say on the matter of our new partnership than either of them would, but now wasn't the time. "No, all of it can wait. We can talk later."

"And who put you in charge?" Violet asked, her brow furrowing.

I was done.

I dropped Joe's arm and pointed my finger in her face. "*I* made me in charge. Unless Joe donated a ton more money than I think he did, I'm the majority owner of the nursery. And Violet, since you didn't contribute any money, that makes you an *employee*."

Her jaw slacked. "What?"

"And as your *boss*, I'm giving you the day off. Go home, Violet."

She shook her head, her anger returning. "You can't do that!"

"I just did! Go!"

She stood and grabbed her purse off the only free space on the sales counter. "This isn't over, Rose Anne Gardner."

"I never said it was. I said it could wait. Now *go*."

Violet started to leave, then spun around. "But consider this, Rose: How much are you helping him right now and how much are you hurtin'?"

I gritted my teeth but didn't answer. Her words echoed my own thoughts, but I trusted my heart and my heart told me to stay.

After Violet walked out the door, I turned to Joe. "I can go. I just didn't want to leave you alone in Violet's claws right now."

"Please stay." He grabbed my hand and we sat side by side, our fingers intertwined as we stared at the rubble of what remained of my business—now his too, it would seem. I found it amazing how less than ten minutes ago I had been furious with him, and now I was sharing in his pain.

"Maybe she's lying," I whispered after half a minute of silence.

He sucked in his lower lip and shook his head, looking down at the floor. "No. She's not. I can tell."

"But are you sure it's yours?" Even though he'd slept with her after our breakup, it still hurt to ask the question.

He released a choked laugh, his eyes filling with tears. "Look on the bright side. We can raise our babies together."

I sucked in a breath. "Oh. You don't know."

His head swiveled to face me, worry pinching the corners of his eyes. "Know what?"

"I'm not pregnant."

His eyes sank closed and relief washed over his face, quickly replaced with resignation. He rested his elbow on his leg and covered his face with his free hand. "Are congratulations in order or regrets?"

"Joe."

He stood, shaking his head as he surveyed the destruction around us. "I can't catch a damn break, can I?"

I stood. "Joe."

He spun around and stared at me, heartbreak written all over his face. "I wasn't trying to harass you yesterday, although my behavior lately must have made it look that way." He took a breath. "I'm sure Mason told you about the big bust down by Pickle Junction."

My guts twisted. Mason *had* mentioned it, but he hadn't needed to. I'd been at the underground auction for Daniel Crocker's black market business with Skeeter Malcolm, so I'd seen it all firsthand. "Yeah."

"We didn't know how it was going to shake out. The auction was south of town, but if things went bad, we were worried there'd be some kind of turf war at Weston's Garage, north of town. I wanted to make sure you stayed home. You have a knack for getting in trouble—whether you're looking for it or not—and staying home seemed like the best option for you."

I clenched my hands at my sides and then relaxed them. He was right. I'd thought the worst of him when he was only trying to keep me safe. "I'm sorry." My voice broke.

He gave me a grim smile. "Don't be sorry. You haven't done anything wrong."

"What are you going to do about…"

"Hilary?"

I nodded, feeling nauseated again. "She's got it all planned out."

His eyebrows rose with his smirk. "She always has." He moved toward me, stopping less than a foot away. "Do you believe in destiny, Rose?"

We'd had this conversation before. "You know I do, Joe." My voice broke again.

"I used to too. I used to think you were my destiny." Tears filled his eyes. "Maybe I should put more stock in karma." He swallowed again, the tears threatening to fall. "I haven't been a good person, Rose. I've done some terrible things."

I shook my head. "Maybe so, but I believe that deep in your heart you're a good person, Joe McAllister."

"I know." A tear slid down his cheek. "And you believed in me enough for both of us." He choked on a sob. "Now what do I do?"

I threw my arms around his neck, burying my face into his chest as my own sobs broke loose. "I can't go back to you, Joe. I can't. Especially not now."

His arms wrapped around my back, pulling me flush against him as his body heaved. "I know."

We clung together, crying in each other's arms for nearly a minute until he pulled away. "I love you, Rose, but I'm letting you go for real this time." Then he pulled me back into a hug, squeezing me tight before kissing the top of my head and backing up several steps.

"Are you leaving Henryetta?" I asked, suddenly panicked.

"No." He wiped his cheeks with the back of his hand. "Ironically enough, I feel like I belong here. With or without you."

I nodded.

"We'll discuss the business later." His gaze swept the ruined room again before he walked out the door. "It's not going anywhere."

And neither was Joe. That thought filled me with more relief than I had a right to.

Chapter Two

Rose

I swallowed a fresh sob and wondered what to do. I needed to talk to someone, but who? Mason was tied up with work at the courthouse. He'd barely had time to talk to me earlier, when I'd called to tell him about my doctor's visit. I went with the next person who popped into my head. Someone I could always count on to support me and give me sound, unbiased advice.

Jonah's secretary gave me an anxious glance when I walked into the office of the New Living Hope Revival Church. Poor Jessica had her sights set on Reverend Jonah Pruitt, and she'd seen me as a threat ever since starting her position a couple of months ago. Her anxiety had lessened after she learned that Mason and I were together, but I suspected no one spent as much time behind closed doors with Jonah as I did.

"Hi, Jessica." I glanced at the closed office door. "Is Jonah busy?"

"He can't see you right now," she said, her mouth pursed. "He's with someone."

"Okay." My nerves were wound up tighter than a ball of yarn, but I wasn't about to take advantage of my friendship with my pastor if he was genuinely busy. "Do you know how much longer he's going to be?"

She gave me a half-shrug. "Not sure."

I wanted to assure her that I wasn't her enemy, that I was actually trying to help her cause, but I would never betray Jonah's trust. Instead, I said, "Would you tell him I was here and I'll—?"

Jonah's door swung open and the voices of the two men in the doorway filled the reception area. The middle-aged man across from Jonah shook his hand. "Thanks, Reverend."

Jonah gave him a grin. "Now, Phil. I thought we'd agreed you would call me Jonah."

"Well, thank you, Jonah. I'll see you on Sunday."

Jonah's gaze followed his visitor toward the door, then landed on me. "Rose, to what do I owe this pleasure..." His voice broke off when he saw the tears that were already filling my eyes. He reached out for me and looked over his shoulder. "Jessica, hold all my calls."

He ushered me into his office, then shut the door behind us before guiding me to the guest chair in front of his desk. I was glad I didn't have to see the look on Jessica's face.

"When are you going to ask that poor girl out?" I asked, reaching for a tissue off his desk. "You'd make my life a whole lot easier."

"I'm working on it." He sat next to me, the barest hint of a grin lifting his mouth. Jonah Pruitt was a good-looking man. He put more care into his appearance than most men, but if I had my own weekly televised service,

I'd probably do the same. His short blond hair was gelled and spiked in a way that suited him. The truth was, he could have his pick of just about any single woman under the age of forty in Fenton County and beyond, but his past love-life experiences hadn't ended so well. Which was, of course, an understatement given that his mother had murdered his old girlfriend.

I blew my nose into the tissue. "Well, work on it faster."

"Rose, what's going on?"

Tears filled my eyes again. "I don't even know where to start."

He gave me a sympathetic smile. "It's usually best if you start at the beginning."

"I'm a terrible person, Jonah. If you were a priest, I'd be making a long confession."

He chuckled. "You, a terrible person? Not likely. But tell me what you've done if it'll make you feel better."

I took a deep breath. "You know that big bust at the barn outside of Pickle Junction city limits…?"

His smile fell. "Yeah…"

"Did you hear that all the money was returned to the businesses that had been robbed?"

Now he looked downright scared. "Yeah…"

I tucked my legs on the seat, under my skirt. "I might know what happened."

"And do I want to how you came to know it?"

My eyes met his. "Are we protected by client-psychologist confidentiality?"

His gaze leveled with mine. "What did you do?"

"Nothing bad. Not really. I just kept Skeeter Malcolm from getting killed, and in return he helped me get my money back."

His eyes widened and his voice rose. "You're the Lady in Black."

"Shh!" I leaned over the arm of my chair. "No one can know, Jonah!"

"You really are?"

I didn't answer, which I knew would be confirmation enough.

"Joe and Mason didn't figure out it was you?"

"No, thank God."

Jonah shook his head in disbelief. "I didn't suspect, so I guess they wouldn't either. How'd you get mixed up with Skeeter Malcolm anyway?"

"It's a long story." I shifted in my seat.

He sat back in his chair. "Good thing I don't have another appointment for an hour and a half."

"How'd you know about The Lady in Black and Skeeter?" Neely Kate already knew, but she often knew things people never ever found out about. I'd been hoping this would be the same.

"*Every*body knows you were with Skeeter. Well, not *you*. The Lady in Black."

"Great," I grumbled, sinking deeper into the chair. "I told him it was a stupid name."

"I'm waiting. How did it happen?"

"After I figured out that the guys who robbed the bank were planning to bid for Daniel Crocker's business, which Skeeter was the only real contender to win, I figure he might appreciate knowing about his competition."

Jonah scowled. "You were supposed to take that information to Mason, not Skeeter Malcolm."

I placed my hands on the arms of the chair. "You know I needed the money by today to save the business. If I'd told Mason, I wouldn't have gotten it back in time. If at all." I knew I sounded defensive. I supposed I was.

He took a deep breath and released it. "I still don't get how you ended up at the auction."

"When I went to Skeeter to see if he was interested in the exchange, I didn't stop to think that he'd want to know *how* I knew." I grimaced. "Skeeter got really ticked off, so Bruce Wayne panicked and told him about my visions."

"Wait." Jonah sat up and leaned toward me. "How did Bruce Wayne get involved in this? I didn't realize he knew about your visions."

"I never told him, Jonah." I sighed. "He figured it out on his own. Go figure. And once I got it in my head to get Skeeter's help, Bruce Wayne called Scooter to set up the meeting."

Jonah shook his head, frowning. "Rose, do you understand the seriousness of what you've done? If Bruce Wayne got caught up in any of that—"

"I know, Jonah. I know. I told him I was going to do it without him, but he refused to help unless he let him come with me. He insisted the business was worth fighting for. So I made him a partner."

"A partner? In your business?"

I nodded. "I'm going to split up the business and Bruce Wayne and I are going to be co-owners of the landscaping portion."

"Are you sure?"

"It's just as much his business as it is mine. I may be putting up the money, but I wouldn't be this successful without him. Especially now."

He nodded. "Let's jump forward. How did you end up at the auction?"

"Once Skeeter realized I had the sight, he made me have a vision. I saw him get murdered at the auction."

"So he made you go to see if it would change?"

"Yeah, but I insisted on wearing a disguise. I saved Skeeter but then the auction was busted. I panicked when I heard Joe's voice shouting orders, but Skeeter and Jed got away through a trapdoor and took me with them."

Jonah was silent for several moments, making me uncomfortable. "So you got your money back and saved your business?"

"I didn't get my money back at the auction. I found it on my front porch last night." I cringed. "And I didn't use it to save my business because it had already been saved."

He shook his head in confusion. "Wait? Was it Mason? Did he find the money after all? But why did you go through with the auction then?"

"It wasn't Mason." I paused. "It was Joe. He and Violet were in cahoots and Joe paid off my loan at the bank on Wednesday. That's why they were spending so much time together. Planning it all, I guess."

He continued to watch me. "What did Mason say when you told him?"

"He doesn't know yet. I only found out right before I came to see you. Vi asked me to meet her at the nursery at eleven and Joe was there in his uniform." I rubbed my forehead, fighting more tears. "Joe put a lot of work into getting the nursery ready this summer. He said he couldn't let it die. So when Violet told him about our money troubles, he offered to help. He's a partial owner now."

Jonah was still for several seconds. "How does one woman get herself into so many predicaments?"

I grabbed another tissue off the desk and blew my nose. "I have no idea."

"You'll need to verify this with Mason, but I doubt Joe can claim a stake in your business. Even if he did pay off the debt, he's not a legal owner. It's still yours."

I nodded, still unsure what to make of the whole mess. "There's something else."

"There's *more*?" He looked horrified. "Sorry."

I offered him a grim smile. "Hilary showed up at the nursery this morning, looking for Joe." I paused, trying to push the words past the lump in my throat. "She's pregnant."

Jonah's face paled.

"And I'm not. I took a test last night and went to the doctor this morning so he could confirm it." I lifted my eyebrows. "And before you ask how I feel about that, I'm equally relieved and disappointed. Which confuses me."

"It's understandable. You were preparing yourself for a baby and had probably convinced yourself it could be a good thing."

"Well, my vision about Hilary is coming true." The night before Joe and I broke up, I'd had a vision of Joe winning an election with a very pregnant Hilary at his side.

"No," Jonah said. "Big elections are in November, and yesterday was Thanksgiving. Unless Hilary has become an elephant without us realizing it, the timing is off."

"Does it matter when she's due, Jonah?" I asked. "Pregnant is pregnant."

"True, but you're with Mason now, so why does it bother you so much?"

My chin quivered. "I asked myself the same question. Part of it was that she told him in front of me and Violet, and Joe just looked so blindsided and devastated. I've never seen him that way. Not even when he broke up with me."

"And the other part?"

"Joe and I are better off apart, but I care about him. I don't like it that he's hurting right now."

Jonah's hand covered mine. "You are a remarkably good person, Rose Gardner. Most people wouldn't feel that way about their exes."

"Maybe it's because it was a mutual split. We didn't break up out of hatred or a lack of love; we did it to save each other." I looked into Jonah's eyes. "Will you talk to him?"

"Joe?"

I nodded. "He's dealing with this whole issue with Hilary, and I think he's finally accepted that I'm not going back to him. He needs to talk to someone, someone who's not me."

"I'm not exactly Joe Simmons' favorite person, but I'll reach out to him and see if he's receptive. It's the best I can do, Rose."

I leaned over the arm of the chair and hugged him. "And it's all I can ask. Thank you."

I started to get up but Jonah pulled me back down to the chair. "What are you going to tell Mason?"

"I'll tell him about Joe saving the business and get his take on that and on Hilary."

"I'm not worried about those parts. I'm talking about the Lady in Black."

I shook my head. "No. I'm not telling him. I helped Skeeter at the auction and I got my money. It's done."

"What do you think Mason will say when he finds out you helped Skeeter Malcolm become the new crime boss of Fenton County? Mason can't stand Skeeter; he's vowed to bring him down."

I squared my shoulders. "Then I have all the more reason *not* to tell him."

"Rose."

"I have to go, Jonah." I hopped out of the chair and took a step backward, out of his reach. "It's done. Who cares about the Lady in Black? She made one appearance and now she's gone forever."

"I think you're being naïve."

I suspected Jonah was right, but Mason and I were still recovering from a few speed bumps. I didn't want to add kindling to a smoldering fire. "I'll wait until the time is right."

"The longer you wait, the harder it's going to be."

"I'll think about it." I bolted for the door and opened it as Jonah reached me.

"You know I care about you, Rose," Jonah said, wrapping me into a hug.

"I care about you too, Jonah." I pushed up on my tiptoes to kiss him on the cheek, catching the livid stare of his secretary. "Are you really interested in Jessica?" I whispered in his ear.

His ears flushed. "Well, yeah…"

I broke from his embrace. "Jonah, what are you doing tonight?" I said loudly.

"Well…I was going to go home and watch TV."

I turned to his secretary. "Jessica, Jonah would love to invite you to dinner, but he's too shy to ask. Would you be interested in going out with him tonight?"

Her cheeks turned pink and she scrunched her shoulders up to her ears. "Yes."

"Jonah, where would you like to go?"

"Uh… Jasper's…"

I grinned. "Good choice." Of course, it was really one of the only choices here in Henryetta. "Jessica, Jonah will pick you up at seven."

I walked out of the office, leaving two stunned people behind. Before I got into my truck, my phone dinged with a text.

That was a Neely Kate move, Jonah sent.

I laughed, then texted back, *I'll take that as a compliment.*

Thank you

<3

My smile quickly fell when I realized where I needed to go next.

Mason's office.

Chapter Three

Rose

Mason's office was bustling with activity when I walked in. His secretary glanced up at me with a flustered look. "He's really busy, Rose."

"That's okay," I said leaning to the side to take a peek through his open door.

Mason was sitting on the edge of his desk, his broken leg extended in front of him. An older man in a suit and two men in sheriff's uniforms were in his office with him. I recognized two of the men and my heart leaped into my throat. One was the sheriff, Mervin Foster, and the other was Mason's boss: George Hanover, Fenton County District Attorney. There was no sign of Joe, which was strange, since he was the sheriff's second-in-command.

The four of them were deep in conversation.

Mason turned his head slightly and noticed me standing by his secretary's desk. He held up a finger and said something to the other men before grabbing his cane and hobbling out to see me.

"Mason, you didn't have to come out here," I whispered.

He grabbed my arm and tugged me around a corner to a small break room. "I wanted to see you after you went to the doctor. Is he sure you're okay?"

"I'm fine. You didn't need to worry."

"I love you, so that makes it my job to worry."

I smiled up at him.

"I'm sorry, but it looks like I'll have to be here all day. I'd much rather be with you and my mother, but we're still dealing with the fallout from that bust yesterday."

My heart jolted. "Oh?"

"We're at a loss. We were hoping to arrest Skeeter Malcolm at that barn. We heard he was there, but we think he got away through a door that led to an underground tunnel."

I quirked an eyebrow, trying to look surprised. "Oh."

"But what's really got us perplexed is this mystery woman who was with him." He lowered his voice. "We're trying to figure out who she is and where she came from."

"You don't say." I forced myself to stay calm. "What does it matter?"

"Because we think Malcolm has taken over Crocker's empire. Crocker was trying to expand his business when he was arrested. If Malcolm has outside influence, it could mean big trouble in Fenton County."

"Oh."

He gave me a strange look. "Are you okay?"

I took a breath to calm down. "I have some things to tell you, but not now. You need to get back to your meeting."

He cast an anxious look down the hall. "I'm sorry, Rose."

I gave him a quick kiss. "It's your job and it's an important one to boot. We'll talk tonight. And then we can spend the day with your mom tomorrow."

He cringed. "Sweetheart, I probably won't be able to go now."

I tried to hide my disappointment. "Oh. It's okay."

"I'm sorry."

"I know. Like I said, your job is important. I'll see you tonight."

I gave him a hug and started to break away, but he tugged me back and cupped my face in his hands. "Rose, I really am sorry. I wanted to spend the day with you."

"I know, but I have to leave now anyway. I need to check on Bruce Wayne."

"I didn't think you had a job today."

I sighed. "We don't, but we need to talk about...things."

"Did you make your payment to the bank? That's another component we're working on. All the missing money just turning up. We haven't even caught the guys who did this."

I wished I could tell him everything now, but he had more important things to do. Like tracking down the Lady in Black and bringing me in for questioning. "I'll tell you all about it when we have some time to talk.

Come on." I tugged on his hand. "Let's get you back to that room full of very important Fenton County officials."

I dropped my hold when we neared his office door and he caught me by surprise, wrapping an arm around my back and pulling me close. His mouth lowered to mine and he kissed me until my knees were weak. When he lifted his head, his eyes pleaded with mine. "Don't give up on me, Rose."

"I should be the one saying that," I said, my guilt getting the better of me.

He lowered his mouth to my ear. "I'm very nearly over what happened between you and Joe last week. Stop worrying."

At the moment, my kiss with Joe seemed like the least of my worries. I forced a smile. "Get back to work before someone sees us, Mr. Prosecutor."

"I'll call you later."

"I love you, Mason."

"I love you too."

I went down to the first floor and found Neely Kate at her desk looking peaked.

"Neely Kate, you really need to get to the doctor," I said, leaning against the counter.

She looked up from her papers and grinned. "I have an appointment this afternoon, thank you very much." She got up and walked over to the counter. "How'd it go with Violet and Joe?"

"This is a conversation that will take some time. Have you been to lunch?"

"No, I was going to skip it because of my appointment, but I can go now."

"Are you sure?"

"Please," she said, walking over to her desk and opening a drawer to get her purse. "You know I try to get away from this place any chance I can get. Besides, Rachel is in the back." Neely Kate leaned to the side and yelled to the back area crowded with file cabinets and shelves, "Rachel, I'm going to lunch!"

"Okay," her coworker grumbled.

Neely Kate seemed to be the only Fenton County employee who didn't walk around with a permanent bad attitude. Well, except for Mason, whose disposition had improved greatly after we started spending time together as friends in September.

"Merilee's?" she asked as she slipped her arms into her coat.

"Are you sure you're up to it?"

"Pfft." She waved her hand as though I was talking nonsense. "Let's go."

We walked across the street through the snowflakes that were blowing around again.

"I didn't realize snow was in the forecast," Neely Kate murmured.

"Maybe it will help sell all those live Christmas trees on our lot."

She opened the door to the restaurant and turned back to look at me. "How'd you pay for those trees? Did Skeeter give you a loan?"

"Let's get inside and I'll tell you."

After we sat down and ordered, I told Neely Kate about Joe's financial commitment to the nursery. I knew she was dying to know about what had happened at the auction, but neither one of us would dream of talking about it here. It was where everyone in the courthouse went to eat, so it was about as far from private as we could get.

"So the business is safe?" she asked.

"And then some. Joe not only paid what we owed, but also the balance of the loan."

"Wow. What'd you say when you found out?"

"I told them both I quit."

She gave her head a shake. "How's that gonna work since you own at least seventy percent?"

"I don't know. We never had a chance to sort it out. Hilary showed up and dropped a bombshell."

Her eyebrows rose at the mention of Hilary's name. "I'm scared to ask what that might be," she said after a moment.

I folded my hands together on the table. "She's pregnant."

Her mouth formed an O. "Poor Joe."

"I know. He was devastated. She wants to get married in a few weeks on their original wedding date. She said her mother never cancelled any of the plans."

She puckered her mouth. "Well, *that's* enlightening. He broke up with her, yet she didn't cancel the fake wedding. Then she turns up when it's only a few weeks away and claims she's pregnant. How convenient." She drew out the last word as thick as molasses in January.

"I think she really might be pregnant, Neely Kate. She showed Joe a paper with the lab results."

Neely Kate didn't look impressed. "Anyone with a computer can fake that."

"That's what Joe insinuated. But then she told him she made an appointment at the doctor's office this afternoon. She's scheduled an ultrasound so Joe can see the baby's heartbeat."

"Oh, dear. She can't fake *that*." She put her hand over mine. "How are *you* handling all of this?"

Her question caught me off guard. "Better and worse than I expected."

She shook her head. "That makes no sense."

"I know." I tucked a loose strand of hair behind my ear and leaned closer, lowering my voice. "I'm upset, but it's not because I'm jealous, although I do feel weird when I think about it. But I'm mostly upset for Joe. I just feel incredibly sad to see him linked to her in such a permanent way. I know he got himself into this situation, but I don't want him to pay for it when the price is so high."

"Why shouldn't he pay for his mistake?" my friend asked, taking a sip of her water. "When has Joe Simmons ever paid for *any* of his mistakes or learned from them?"

"He paid for *many* mistakes when he lost me," I whispered. "No matter what you think, I know for a fact it broke Joe's heart to leave me." I cleared my throat. "But you're right, he still hasn't learned. After he came back to town, he tried to get me back even though his daddy still has all his incriminating evidence on us. And as far as I could tell, he had no plans to rectify the situation. Still"—I looked up into Neely Kate's eyes, pleading with her to understand—"I would never wish this situation on him, and most certainly not on a tiny baby."

"You're right. No one—especially a baby—deserves to live with that witch."

"I asked Jonah to talk to Joe."

"You did *what*? Joe can't stand him."

"Well, Jonah's gonna try anyway. He's all alone, Neely Kate. He needs a friend."

"You are not responsible for Joe's misery. I know you feel bad for him, but he needs to sort this out on his own. He's your *ex*-boyfriend, Rose. Let it go."

"I still care about him, Neely Kate. You know he'd be there to help me in a heartbeat. He's already proven that with Daniel Crocker. Several times."

"He did that to win you back."

I shook my head. "Yes, but he would have helped me anyway."

"You need to leave this alone, Rose," Neely Kate hissed. "What's Mason gonna say if he finds out you're giving comfort to Joe Simmons? Especially after he kissed you? And not to mention you need to worry about Mason finding out about…*other things*."

I took a deep breath, leaning close and whispering so no one else could hear. "He's in his office right now with the DA, the sheriff, and somebody else. They're trying to figure out the identity of the woman who was at the auction with Skeeter Malcolm."

"Oh, crap," Neely Kate said louder than I liked.

"Shh!" I looked around to see if anyone was paying attention to us, but thankfully most of the patrons today were holiday shoppers and not courthouse employees. "No kidding."

"What are you going to do?" she whispered.

I grimaced with a half shrug. "Hope it all goes away...?"

Her eyes narrowed with irritation. "You need to tell Mason you were there."

"And what's he gonna say to *that*, Neely Kate? He would be furious."

She leaned her forearms on the table, her face a foot from mine as she whispered, "You should have thought about that before you went to Skeeter in the first place."

"I never expected any of *this* to happen!" I still kept my voice low. "Besides, if I were to tell Mason about my association with...Skeeter, I'd incriminate him, and I can't do that."

"Why on earth not?"

"Because he helped me, Neely Kate. I went to him in good faith and I can't betray him now."

"Then you're good and stuck, aren't you?"

I put my elbow on the table, resting my chin on my hand and grumbled, "So what else is new?"

After lunch, I needed to call Bruce Wayne, but there was someone I had to talk to first. Violet.

Chapter Four

Violet

I *hated* the house I'd grown up in. The day I left to marry Mike a few months after high school graduation was the happiest day of my life. Or so I thought at the time.

Only I'd gone from one form of oppression to another.

Since moving back in several weeks ago, I had spent nearly every minute cleaning the tiny nine-hundred square foot home, trying to scrub away the bad memories to no avail. Rose had redecorated most of the surfaces after Momma died, putting up fresh paint and airy curtains, but it was like slapping a designer dress on a two-bit hooker. The surface might look pretty, but the character underneath was still seedy and coarse.

God, I hated this house.

Ashley hadn't taken my separation from Mike well, and she often woke up in the middle of the night in tears. But my daughter's nightmares had increased since moving out of the only home she'd ever known…and so had my anxiety. I'd sit up in bed in a cold sweat, roused by her screams, reliving the ugly hateful past, Rose's cries mingling with Ashley's in my head.

"Violet! Help me!"

Holding my little girl in the darkness reminded me of holding another little girl, smoothing her hair and telling her it was okay.

"Don't leave me, Violet," she'd plead through her tears.

I promised that I never would. Ever.

And I hadn't.

I'd always stayed close to protect her from the woman who had called herself our mother. Three years after our wedding, Mike was offered a job in Little Rock. His father's construction business was struggling at the time, so he'd begged me to move. I refused. Daddy had died only months before and Momma had insisted Rose come home from college, leaving in the middle of the second semester of her first year. I'd tried to talk Rose out of coming home to Henryetta, but Momma had my baby sister wrapped good and tight in her cycle of abuse, and Rose came running back desperate for Momma's love and approval, despite the fact I'd spent the majority of my life trying to give her the love our mother refused her.

I couldn't remember a time when I hadn't protected her. One of my earliest memories was of four-year-old Rose standing in the living room crying while Momma leaned over her, shouting, "You're an evil child! I'll beat that demon right out of ya!" But instead of beating her, Momma stuffed her in the hall closet and shut the door. That punishment was far more effective than any beating ever could be.

Rose was terrified of being trapped in enclosed spaces.

My little sister screamed and cried in terror while I pleaded with Momma to let her out. Instead, Momma sent me to my room and told me to stay out of it. I sat on the floor of the stuffy bedroom Rose and I shared, staring at the closet door across the hall. My own tears slid down my face as I listened to my little sister cry. I had learned that any attempts to help her would only make her punishment worse, so I just sat there in our stuffy room, sweat dripping down my back, making my cotton shirt stick to my skin. Within fifteen minutes, Rose's cries turned to soft whimpers and I heard a knock at the front door.

"What's all the ruckus, Agnes?" Miss Mildred asked through the screen door.

"Rose," was all Momma said, but the "hmm" Miss Mildred released said she knew all about my little sister and her *devious* behavior.

The screen door banged open then shut, and I could hear their muffled voices as they gossiped about Miss Opal, who lived across the street. Poking my head out of the bedroom door, I realized they were on the front porch, sitting in Momma's wicker chairs.

My stomach knotted into a tight ball as I ran across the hall into the bathroom and filled a small cup with water. Making sure Momma was still outside, I opened the closet door and found Rose on the floor, huddled against the wall. Strands of her dark brown hair were plastered to her damp, reddened cheeks and her eyes blinked at the sunlight.

"Violet?" she whimpered.

I turned to look toward the front door, panicked that Momma would discover what I was doing and hurt us even worse. "Here." I thrust the cup at her and she grabbed it, gulping the water in a matter of seconds.

"Come back later," Momma said, still outside. "I've got a pot of beans goin'."

My heart began to race. "Stop cryin', Rose, and Momma will let you out."

"I'm scared, Vi." Her voice broke and fresh tears filled her eyes.

"I know." I swallowed down my fear and took the cup from her. "Pretend I'm holdin' your hand. Okay?" I grabbed her hand and gave it a quick squeeze before shutting the door and scurrying to my room and landing on my bed. I heard the door bang against the frame and the floorboards creak as Momma walked to the closet door. I stuffed the cup under my pillow.

Momma asked, "Have you learned your lesson, girl?"

I held my breath when I didn't hear anything, then Momma's voice rose, "Speak up, you evil child. *Have you learned your lesson?*"

"Yes, Momma." I could barely hear her answer.

"Get in yer room and stay there until your father comes home," Momma barked.

Seconds later, Rose stood in the doorway, her cotton dress soaked with sweat. I jumped off the bed we shared and grabbed her hand, leading her to the part of the mattress that was in front of the open window. A soft breeze blew the curtains, but I could hardly feel it, so I lifted Rose's hair off her neck and blew on her to help cool her off. She began to cry again, silent tears falling down her face, and my heart ached in sympathy.

I hadn't saved her from our mother's wrath. The only thing I could do now was comfort her.

"What did you see this time?" I whispered. It was always the things Rose saw in her head that got her into trouble.

"Momma dropped a hamburger on the floor and then gave it to Daddy."

"Oh, no." Of course, it wasn't the seeing that was the problem. It was the fact that she always recounted what it was she'd seen. She'd told Momma about that burger falling. "You have to make it stop, Rose."

"I don't know how." Her voice quivered with her tears.

I hated our mother and I hated Daddy for letting Momma treat Rose that way. But sometimes—usually when Momma was in a hate-filled rage—I hated Rose too, for her stupid visions that made our lives hell, even though I knew she couldn't stop them.

When Rose started school, it wasn't long before the other kids figured out she was different. But Henryetta's elementary school was small enough that I could track down each and every kindergartner who dared to be mean to my sister. Maybe I couldn't do a thing to stop Momma, but I did my darnedest to keep anyone else from hurting her.

"You can't tell anyone about your visions, Rose," I coached her one day after school, bandaging her knee in our tiny bathroom. A boy in her class had pushed her down at recess. "People will think you're different."

She looked up at me with wide, innocent eyes. "But they already think I'm different, Violet."

I shook my head, dabbing the scrape with a washrag. "Maybe so, but don't give 'em any more ammunition to use against you."

She flinched in pain, then her little nose scrunched with confusion. "What does that mean?"

"It means keep to yourself and don't let anyone hurt you."

I took my own advice and wore it like a shield over my heart. I was the good Gardner sister. The pretty blond-haired, blue-eyed girl who was sweet to everyone. She did her homework, helped her neighbors, and most of all, she obeyed. She was the girl who everyone loved, the one who made up for the disappointment of her younger sister. But I didn't let anyone get close. Through Rose, I learned that people weren't to be trusted. They hurt you and used you and the best way to get through life was to fit in as best as you possibly could.

But even though she had every reason to do otherwise, Rose trusted and saw the good in everyone. One afternoon when I was in sixth grade and she was in fourth, she was crying on the bus when I boarded it.

I slid in next to her, anger burning in my chest. "What happened now?"

Her sad hazel eyes looked up at me. "Nothing."

"Then why are you crying?" I reached for her face, wiping the tears off her cheeks.

Her mouth twisted to the side as she looked down at her lap. "Jenny Blakely tricked me."

"What did she do?"

"She asked me if I wanted to sit with her at lunch, so I did. She wanted my cookie, so I gave it to her after she told me she wanted me to be her new best friend. But at recess she said I was stupid if I believed she could be friends with a freak."

I knew that Jenny was one of the popular girls in the fourth grade and I also knew she had a mean streak. It must have been hereditary because her older sister Maggie—who happened to be in my class—had one too. But while I knew how to handle mean girls, gullible Rose didn't have a clue. "Rose, why did you believe her?"

She looked up at me with her trusting eyes. "Why wouldn't she want to be my friend?"

I talked Momma into letting me make cookies that night so long as I cleaned up my mess and the rest of the kitchen while I was at it. When she wasn't looking, I put laxatives in a small batch of the dough, keeping it separate from the rest. I packaged the special cookies up in individual sandwich bags, using a marker on the plastic to address them to Jenny and a handful of other kids who had been mean to Rose. Then, to make sure their troubles wouldn't be tied back to my sister, I packaged undoctored cookies for the other fifteen students in her class. I put them all into a small brown bag decorated with ribbons and gave them to Rose. "Hand these out to everyone in your class, but be sure to give them to the right people."

"Thank you, Vi." She threw her arms around my neck, squeezing tight. "Everyone's really gonna like me after this."

Poor Rose. She was so sweet and kind, it never occurred to her that other people might not be. Especially her own sister.

That was the irony of it all. Rose was the good one, and I was the wicked one. Seeking revenge and retaliation all while I had the sweetest of smiles on my face. No one ever suspected a thing, least of all Rose.

By the time I was in high school, I'd mastered the art of manipulation. But by then my use of it had expanded beyond defending my sister. It also came in handy for my own personal gain. Mike Beauregard was one year ahead of me, but I decided he was my ticket out of my personal hell called home. He was everything I hoped to have and more. He was the quarterback on the football team. He was smart and popular. His dad owned a business in town and he planned to join it, which meant he'd stick around, allowing me to stay close to Rose. He was dating Stephanie Miller when I decided he would be mine, but it wasn't hard to make him think she was cheating on him. A small part of me felt guilty for that, but that guilt quickly faded when Stephanie found a new boyfriend within a couple of weeks.

I was already popular, but dating Mike raised me to a higher status. I was Homecoming Queen my senior year and I was happy, or as happy as I was capable of being with my stone cold heart.

After I graduated, I got a job with an insurance agent while Mike had been working for his dad the past year. Mike didn't seem to be in a hurry to get married—even though we'd discussed it—so I *accidentally* got pregnant to speed things along. Rose was in high school and Momma had gotten even meaner. I reasoned if I married Mike and moved out, I could bring Rose with me and ultimately save her from the witch.

Imagine my surprise when Rose refused to go along with my plan. Mike and I had had a hell of a knock-down, drag-out fight over it after our wedding. All for nothing.

"Momma needs me, Violet," she insisted.

"Momma needs a punching bag and that's you, Rose." I cupped her cheek. "Please. I worry about you now that I'm not there to protect you."

She slowly shook her head, her scraggly hair shaking with it. "I can't leave her." I saw the longing in her eyes. She wanted our mother to love her, but it was never gonna happen. No matter how hard she tried.

"You can. And you must. Please, Rose. You'll have your own room and everything."

I could see the conflict waging in her pretty hazel eyes. "I have my own room anyway ever since you left." She gave me a tiny smile, trying to make me feel better.

I wanted to grab her and shake her. I was the worldly one. I was the one who knew how to protect her. And she always listened to my advice…except when it came to our mother. "Then at least let me take you shopping this Saturday. I'm gonna need some maternity clothes before you know it." I tugged on the sleeve of her oversized shirt. "I got a bonus at work and we can make a day of it. Maybe go to Little Rock? You've never been. It'll be fun."

Her face lit up, then just as quickly faded. "I can't. Momma wants me to deep clean the house."

Anger riled up inside me, but I'd learned from experience that getting angry with Rose never worked. Cajoling was her trigger. "That tiny house doesn't need much cleaning." I tucked a strand of hair behind her ear. "How about I talk to Momma? Then you won't be the one to get in trouble. I'll tell her I'm scared to go by myself. Which wouldn't be a lie," I added to ease her guilt. "I really *would* be scared to go alone."

The happiness bursting from my baby sister's face nearly broke me. How could our Momma do this to her? "Would you?"

I threw my arms around her. "Of course. I love you, Rose. You're the best thing in my life."

"Other than Mike, of course," she said into my shoulder.

Oh, yeah. "Well, of course other than Mike, silly."

It took a lot of finagling to get Momma to agree to the trip, but she finally did. And then on Friday afternoon, while I sat at my desk at Seton Insurance

Agency, I started bleeding and lost my baby. I was thirteen weeks along.

Rose came over and spent the weekend, taking care of me and cooking for Mike. Thankfully, Mike loved her. Truth be told, he would have been history long before then if he didn't. He just hated that I spent so much time consumed over her. Rose was a thorn in our relationship. One I refused to pull out.

Instead, it festered.

But for all the people who whispered and snickered behind her back about her being a freak, the few people who truly got to know her loved her. How could they not?

While I was sad about losing the baby, part of me was relieved. How could I manage to watch out for Rose if I had my own children to take care of?

During Rose's senior year—after she got accepted to college—I realized I was about to be alone and purposeless. Mike and I weren't getting along, and I was suddenly terrified. I'd done everything for Rose up until now. If she escaped Momma's grasp, she wouldn't need me anymore. But I'd given up any chance of an education when I married Mike and all I knew was what I'd picked up at the insurance agency. How could I live alone off that? Besides, a divorce wasn't acceptable. A divorce would mean failure, and Violet Mae Gardner Beauregard did not *do* failure.

The answer to saving my marriage was as simple as what had led to it in the first place.

A baby.

I got pregnant and had Ashley. My love for her caught me by surprise. That my heart had room enough to love my baby and my sister. And of course, Rose left college and returned home not long after beginning, adding to my worry. Only having Ashley didn't fix anything between Mike and me. It made things worse. I insisted we couldn't raise our baby in the ramshackle rental house where we lived, so Mike took extra work so we could make the down payment on a brand-new house at the edge of town. It worried me to be a little farther away from Rose, who had already moved back home, but she had a job and was using Daddy's old car to get around.

Mike and his dad's business had hit a rough patch, and the new house was a stretch on our budget. Mike was under a lot of pressure to provide for us, especially since he'd insisted I quit my job to take care of our baby. Then, about a year later, he got that job offer in Little Rock. Part of me was dying to go. To leave behind all the bad memories of this town. But I could never, ever leave the one person who truly loved me, no matter what.

Rose.

So we stayed, and Mike resented me for it, even though he knew the reason why. Even though he loved her too.

"Rose is twenty years old, Violet. She's a grown woman. You were married and pregnant with Ashley at twenty. You have to stop smothering her."

It only proved to me that he didn't know her at all. Rose was too pure, too tender-hearted, too naïve to maneuver the world on her own. She needed me.

So we stayed and I put extra effort into making the perfect house for him, being the perfect wife. We had another baby so I could give him a son—didn't every man want a son?—and Mike finally seemed happy with the life I'd made for us.

Only I was utterly miserable.

If only I could get Rose married off to some sweet man, someone who would be gentle and kind to her. Someone I could trust to take care of her so I could be free of the burden. But she looked like a mini-Momma with her baggy clothes, no makeup, and unstyled hair. Add in the fact that she spouted out the most bizarre statements out of nowhere and most people thought she was unbalanced. Which meant no man in his right mind was even interested in her. What was I gonna do?

And then Momma died. And *everything* changed. Only not for the better.

When Momma died, it was as though Rose's chains fell off—which was a good thing—but the whole town was talking. Everyone was certain my sister had killed the witch and I wouldn't have blamed her if she had. God knew the woman had done enough harm to deserve it. But I couldn't deal with the rumors, the people whispering behind my back—and hers. It didn't help matters that Rose chose then, of all times, to finally free herself of Momma's rules. She went shopping and got new clothes that showed off her figure, and Aunt Bessie

cut her hair and showed her how to put on makeup—
something I'd been trying to do for years—and she
showed up at our mother's funeral looking like the
beautiful woman I'd always known her to be. But the
moment I saw her—barely recognizing her—I knew the
town was already stringing up the noose to hang her.
Everyone was certain she was guilty, which boiled my
blood.

I chose to ignore that for a few tiny seconds I
thought she might have done it too.

But then she made that stupid list of things she
wanted to do before she was arrested and Joe Simmons—
Joe McAllister then—was only too eager to help.

I knew what he wanted the moment I found him
helping Rose paint the living room after Momma's
murder. Someone like him could never appreciate how
fragile she was. He would just use her and hurt her, only
Rose was too stubborn to listen to me. She thought she
could go from years of oppression to running around
without a safety net.

To my surprise, Joe really cared about her. And
when it turned out he had been undercover all along, I
was shocked when he continued to spend time with my
sister after the case was closed. But I was even more
shocked to discover that after twenty-four years, Rose no
longer needed me. I'd spent my whole life focused on
making sure she was okay. I couldn't simply let her go
now.

After a few months, I came to accept that Joe loved
Rose, even if he hadn't introduced her to his family,

which I knew was a bad sign. One day Joe and I were working on the nursery while Rose ran errands. I stood at the base of the greenhouse, my hands on my hips. "Are you ashamed of my sister, Joe Simmons?" I asked.

He was on the roof, screwing in a piece of Plexiglas. He sat back and looked down at me. "No. Why would you ask me that?" Then a knowing look filled his eyes. "Is this about my family *again*?"

"You being embarrassed of her is the only reason I can think of why you wouldn't let them meet her."

He ran a hand through his hair, looking frustrated. "You don't know my family, Vi. They'll chew her up and spit her out before she even knows what happened. I can't put her through that."

"So you're trying to protect her?"

"*Everything* I do is to protect her."

"You really do love her, don't you? At first I thought she was just a diversion from the city life for you, but now I know it's more than that."

Joe climbed down off the roof. "I have never loved anyone like I love your sister. I'd move heaven and earth for her, and I know you'd do the same. I think that's why we clashed when we first met. We both want the same thing; we just have different ideas about how to go about it."

I crossed my arms and studied him. Maybe he was right.

"Our fighting is only hurting Rose. She's caught in the middle. I know you're worried that I'm going to hurt her, Violet, but I love her. I want to marry her and have a house full of kids. I want to grow old with her and spend the rest of my life making her happy. You just have to trust me."

He had no idea what he was asking. I'd never trusted anyone in my life. But I could tell he was determined, and he'd sure stuck around a lot longer than I'd expected. The nursery had been the solution to two problems for me, one of which was keeping Rose from running off to Little Rock with him and leaving me behind. I wasn't sorry to admit I'd expected Joe Simmons to disappear after that, but he'd proved me wrong again. Maybe he *could* be good to her, despite who his parents were. "I'm holdin' you to it, Joe Simmons. Don't you dare hurt my sister."

He shook his head, solemn like he was taking a vow. "Never."

Less than two months later he left her sobbing on the floor.

But she still hadn't needed me. By then she'd assembled her own group of misfit friends and she seemed to prefer their comfort to mine. I'd spent my entire life protecting and loving Rose, and now she no longer needed nor wanted me. I felt hurt and betrayed. I'd spent most of my life living for her.

And now I had nothing.

No, I had Brody.

Brody MacIntosh was the biggest surprise of my life.

Let's rewind a year. I came up with the idea of the nursery when I realized I needed something besides Rose and my kids to make me happy. Obviously they weren't filling the void, but I needed Mike to be on board with my idea. I wasn't sure how to broach the subject, so I caught him late one Saturday afternoon when he was cleaning the grill, getting ready for our cookout a few hours later.

"Mike," I started, then hesitated. "Are you happy?"

He shrugged. "Pretty much. I've got you and the kids and the business is going well." He looked up at me. "Why do you ask?"

I sucked in a breath. "You know I love flowers."

He looked around our backyard. It was filled with beds of flora. His face softened. "I know that they make you happy. And I'm glad. They're really pretty."

My stomach was in knots. "What if I wanted to do something with flowers?"

He shook his head in confusion. "You make flower arrangements all the time, Vi. What are you talking about?"

I braced my shoulders. "I want to open a nursery."

He blinked. "You mean a daycare?" His face lit up. "That might not be a bad idea. You could watch kids here and bring in extra money. Lord knows we could use it with all the diapers the baby goes through."

"No, Mike. A *floral* nursery."

His smile fell. "A floral nursery?"

I nodded, pushing on. "It might be a good idea."

"Why would you want to start a business, Violet?" he asked, turning back to the grill and scrubbing vigorously. "You've got your hands full with Ashley and the baby."

"I need something *else*, Mike. Don't you ever feel like you need something else?"

He picked up his beer bottle and took a swig. "Yeah, of course I do. I'd love to own a fishing boat, but we can't swing it right now."

"That's not what I'm talking about. Something bigger. I want to be something other than your wife and Ashley and Mikey's mom."

His face darkened. "You are. You're Rose's sister, which seems to take up *more* than enough of your time."

He started to brush past me, but I grabbed his arm. "I haven't been spending as much time with Rose since Mikey came along. You know that."

He stopped, but he still looked angry. "I've tried to give you everything you asked for, Violet, and you're still not happy."

"Will you at least hear me out? I've been thinking about this for quite a while and I've done my research."

He didn't say anything, but he didn't look receptive.

"The closest nursery is in Magnolia, and while there are places around Henryetta that sell flowers, there's not a year-round nursery. We could fill a retail void, and we could also work with builders." I put my hand on his arm, getting excited that he hadn't stopped me yet. "Think about it. You get all the plants you use for landscaping from the nursery in Magnolia. You could get them from my nursery instead."

His forehead wrinkled. "You mean you want to make it part of the construction business?" He shook his head. "I'd have to talk to Dad."

"No. It would be its own business. And I'd sell to *all* the construction companies."

His eyes hardened. "You mean you'd sell to my competition."

"Well…"

He shook his head, his jaw set. "No."

"How can you just say no? Will you at least *think* about it?"

"*No*. Do you have any idea how much money it would cost to set up a nursery? How much money we *don't have*?"

"I can get loans and grants. They have all kinds of things available to women business owners."

Mike's shoulders stiffened. "You're not considered a woman business owner if your husband is part of the business, Vi."

"I know."

His face reddened. "You want to do this without me?"

"It's not how it sounds, Mike."

"I don't care what kinds of loans or grants you get. Do you have any idea how much time it takes to start a new business? We have a *baby*, Violet. Do you really want to put our baby in daycare?" He shook his head. "Why'd you even have Mikey if you wanted to shuffle him off to someone else?"

"That's not it, Mike. I swear." Tears stung my eyes. "I just want something that's mine. Something that gives me a purpose."

Mike leaned forward and grabbed my arm. "You have a house that's yours, Violet. And two kids inside it. They're both yours too. Taking care of the house you wanted so badly and our two kids is your purpose." He dropped his hold, looking at me with a face awash in disappointment. "Get your priorities straight, Violet."

I'd already been unhappy with my marriage, but that conversation destroyed what little love I had left for him. But I couldn't bring myself to let my marriage go. And I couldn't let go of my dream either. Despite what Mike thought, I was sure my idea would work.

So last April, I went to city hall to find out what it took to get a business license, and that's when I ran into Brody MacIntosh, the mayor of Henryetta. I had little Mikey with me, and Brody came out of his office to help me wrangle him while I asked the clerk questions, Brody himself offering some of the answers. When he offered to walk me out to my car to help me with Mikey—doin' his civic duty he said—I knew I should refuse, but I couldn't bring myself to do it. There was something about him that drew me to him. There always had been. I'd known him in high school, or more accurately, I'd studied him. He was several years older and had been dating his current wife. I'd thought what I felt was a silly schoolgirl crush, but talking to him that afternoon made me question all sorts of things about my marriage. So when he opened my car door for me—his light brown hair blowing in the spring breeze and his brown eyes watching me with an appreciative gleam that made my insides flutter—I figured that was the end of it. But it wasn't. Brody gave me his business card and told me to call him anytime I had a question.

I held onto his card for three days, working up the courage to call him, but he called me first, asking if I needed more answers.

I asked a few lame questions just to keep him on the phone. But when I finally stopped he said, "I have a question of my own, Violet."

"Oh?"

"Meet me for lunch next week."

"To talk about my business?" I asked.

"We can talk about that too if you'd like."

Everything in my head screamed *tell him no*! But I liked the way he looked at me that day at city hall. But more importantly, I liked the way I'd felt, some spark I've never felt with Mike. Before I knew what I was doing, I said, "Okay."

We agreed to meet at an Italian restaurant in Magnolia. I arranged for Mike's mother to take care of the kids while I "ran errands". I couldn't look her in the eye when I dropped them off. Multiple times on the drive to Magnolia, I almost turned my car around and drove back home. *It's a business lunch. Nothing more*, I assured myself. And by the time I pulled into the parking lot, I'd convinced myself that our lunch date was perfectly innocent. But when I walked into the restaurant and saw Brody waiting for me in the foyer, I knew exactly what was going to happen. We barely made it through lunch before we left, making out in the parking lot like a couple of teenagers. Brody pulled me into his car and drove to the Quality Inn, where I spent the best three hours of my previously boring life. But when he drove me back to my car, I looked him in the eye and said, "Brody, I can't do this again."

He didn't say anything, simply gave me a tender kiss and pulled back with a gentle smile. "I think you're the best thing that's ever happened to me, Violet Beauregard. Don't take that away."

I told him I couldn't meet him again and then got out of the car. I picked up the kids and had time to prepare dinner before Mike came home.

Later that night, I laid in bed wondering how I'd gotten to this place. *I*, Violet Mae Gardner Beauregard, was an adulteress. What would Momma say? This would have shown her that *I* was the bad Gardner sister and Rose was the good one. That thought was what spurred me to text Brody at two in the morning and tell him that I'd meet him the next Tuesday.

I knew I should stop it. Each and every time, I told myself not to go. It was wrong and sinful to boot. But I liked who I was when I was with Brody. I felt sexy and desirable. He thought I was smart and funny. He not only listened to me, but *wanted* to hear what I had to say. I wasn't Mike's wife or Ashley and Mikey's mother when we were together. I for sure wasn't Rose's sister. The only reason Brody knew anything about Rose was because he came to Momma's visitation and saw her standing next to me.

But by mid-June, Mike had put two and two together. He wanted a separation, and while it hurt to think that I had failed my marriage, I couldn't help feeling a tiny bit excited about my future. By then Rose had agreed to open my nursery with me, and Brody had pledged to leave his wife. I loved Brody MacIntosh and I was certain he loved me too. Other than my children and Rose, I had never really truly loved someone before like that.

Despite my own blooming happiness, I was still jealous of Rose, as hard as that was to admit. She had Joe and an exciting new life and she was happy, truly happy. I was thrilled for her, but she was moving at light-speed and leaving me behind.

Still, it was hard to admit to myself that part of me was a tiny bit happy when Joe broke up with Rose. I figured we could go back to the way things had been, only it would be even better since Momma was gone. Of course, it didn't work out that way. And what was worse, I found out that Joe's father had photos of me and Brody coming out of a motel room. Dated from last spring.

Brody had left his wife by then, but he was worried about the political fallout, so he went back to her, as miserable as he was about it. And I decided perhaps this was God's way of telling me to go back to my husband, as miserable as the thought made me.

And I tried, God knows I tried to salvage our marriage with counseling, but all it took was one phone call from Brody— "God, I miss you, Violet," he'd breathed into the phone. "I lie awake at night thinking about you naked in my arms..."—and I was right back where I started, meeting him in cheap motels.

The nursery was going well by that point. All except for the fact that I'd overextended the business without telling Rose a blessed thing about it. But the loan manager at the Henryetta Bank told me not to worry, and in fact encouraged me to build the business and make a balloon payment after the Holiday Open House I was planning. But then Mr. Sullivan turned up dead and the bank manager suspected him of embezzlement. So not only were we behind on the three payments to the bank, but we were under risk of foreclosure if we didn't pay what we owed by the Friday after Thanksgiving.

I hated to think it, but it was Rose's fault we were in such dire straits. All she had to do was ask Mason to help her out with the money to get us caught up. He was a lawyer, for heaven's sake. He could more than afford to help her, but she refused to even ask. So I was at risk of losing everything—my nursery, Brody, and possibly my kids—all because of Rose's love life and her stubborn pride.

But then Joe moved back to Henryetta and was living next door to me now that I'd lost the house I loved and moved back into Momma's house. And that's when I realized the answer to our prayers.

Joe.

I knew that Joe would help Rose in a heartbeat. He'd put nearly as much work into getting the nursery going as Rose and I had. And he was desperate to get Rose back. He'd risked his life to save her from Daniel Crocker when they weren't even together. Loaning us several thousand dollars to help us catch up on our loan payments and finance a huge Christmas tree order that couldn't be cancelled would be nothing for Joe Simmons, son of J.R. Simmons, the most powerful man in southern Arkansas.

It wasn't hard to bring it up. Ashley and Mikey loved Joe and he seemed lonely and liked spending time with them, so he didn't put up a protest when I asked him to watch them so I could sneak away to meet Brody. All it took was one little "slip" that the nursery was having problems, and Joe leaped at the chance to help. Especially since he was wound up tighter than a drum over the fact Rose had been involved in the bank robbery that had caused all our troubles. He was desperate to help her, especially since he not only didn't trust Mason to do so, but he thought Mason had an agenda of his own to hurt Rose.

And when I compared the two men, I had to admit that I preferred her with Joe. There was no way a man like Mason Deveraux would stick around in Fenton County for long, but Joe was bound and determined to stay. He was the easy choice.

So we made a pact. He'd help us with the nursery—only he wanted to pay off the loan in its entirety and funnel more money into the expansion—and in turn, I'd help him get Rose back.

That was the plan.

But when Rose insinuated that there was no way Joe could be interested in *me*, like I was some second-choice loser, it filled me with rage. Why *wouldn't* Joe be interested in me?

So while my original plan was to make Rose a teensy bit jealous so she'd see how much she wanted Joe back, I changed course. I wanted to make her jealous of me instead. Make her think that I had what she wanted, even if she was too stupid to realize it.

While Joe had agreed to go to Jasper's with me so she'd see us together, hoping it would arouse her curiosity if nothing else, he'd been more reluctant to accept my invitation to church. But he quickly caved when Ashley asked him—all I had to do was make a throwaway comment to her about how nice it would be if Uncle Joe came to church with us.

I'd spent most of my life manipulating people to help Rose. Why stop now?

I knew Rose would initially be upset that Joe was a partial owner of the business. I also knew she'd cool down and realize it was for the best. And with Joe a part of her everyday life, she'd soon realize that he was the man she wanted, not Mason Deveraux, the assistant district attorney who spent most of his time in his office. Mason didn't deserve her. If he really loved her, he'd spend more time with her, just like Joe wanted to do.

But it all went so wrong. Rose was angrier than I expected she be, and then that witch Hilary showed up claiming she was pregnant. I suspected she was lying until she told Joe she'd set up an ultrasound. She might really be pregnant, but I was certain she was carrying someone else's baby…and I was determined to prove it. But I had my work cut out for me since I hadn't handled any of it well. Instead of encouraging Rose to stay with

Joe—since the more time she spent with him the sooner she'd come to her senses—I let my jealousy and spite get in the way of my master plan.

The doorbell rang and I answered the front door, not surprised to see Rose on the porch, her eyes lit up with anger. I had to admit, I liked this new Rose, this girl with more backbone. If only she'd use it for her own good instead of to her detriment. But there was plenty of time to fix that too.

She lifted her chin and squared her shoulders. "Violet, we need to talk."

I tried to hide my smile. "Yes, Rose. We do."

Chapter Five

Rose

My temper had dulled after talking to Neely Kate, but a deeper anger remained. Violet had spent the better part of my adult life manipulating me, only I'd been too blind to see it. This time, she'd gone too far.

I stood on the front porch of the home where I'd spent most my life, feeling like I didn't belong. But Violet didn't either. I cast a glance over to Joe's house and wondered if it would be best if we found her another place to live, for more reasons than one. But then I reminded myself that I was here for a different reason.

I knocked on the front door, preparing myself for a fight. My sister opened the door and I blurted out, "Violet, we need to talk."

She watched me for a second, and I could have sworn I saw pride in her eyes before she said, "Yes, Rose. We do." She stood back and I walked into the house, once again amazed at how Violet could make the house look so good. But then, I suspected Violet could make a swine look good with a little silk and some ribbon. All the decorations she had put up for the open house had transformed our nursery into a beautiful holiday wonderland until Brody's wife trashed it.

"Aunt Rose!" Ashley shouted, launching herself at me.

I dropped to my knees and gave her a big hug. "Ashley, I've missed you."

"You saw me yesterday," she laughed.

"But that was *yesterday*." I gave her a kiss on the cheek and stood. "I hadn't thought about the kids being home. Maybe we should do this another time."

"No," Violet said, "we need to do this now." She looked down at my niece. "Ash, Mommy and Aunt Rose have to talk about important grownup stuff. Since Mikey is taking a nap, why don't you go watch a movie on Mommy's TV? Do you need help?"

Ashley scowled her disgust. "No. I'm not a baby." She walked into the bedroom Violet and I had once shared. It surprised me that Vi hadn't chosen Momma's old bedroom for herself, since it was slightly larger, but I had chosen to stay in the same room after Momma's death. It felt like the only safe place in the house. Maybe it was the same way for Violet.

"Shut the door," Violet called after her, then added, "quietly so you don't wake Mikey."

I heard the little girl grumble before the door closed. "She reminds me so much of you when you were little," I said, becoming nostalgic, my eyes still on the bedroom door. "So strong and independent. I swear, we could have run away from home together when you were her age and we probably would have survived just fine."

"That's funny," Violet said, sounding just as wistful as I felt. "She reminds me so much of you."

"I miss you." My voice broke. "What happened to us?"

Her eyes turned glassy, but she didn't answer.

But I wasn't here for a trip down memory lane. I suspected it was too late for that. "You went too far, Violet. You had no right to ask Joe behind my back to help us with the business." My words lacked the harsh bite of anger. Even I could hear my resignation.

She motioned to the sofa. "Can we sit down? Let me tell you my side of it."

I took a seat on the sofa while she sank into the cushions next to me.

"Rose, you have to know that that nursery is my heart and soul. I lost my marriage and I lost you. Besides Ashley and Mikey, it's all I have left."

"Violet, that's not true."

Her eyebrows rose and she released a bitter laugh. "Isn't it?" She shook her head. "But that's beside the point. All three of us—you, me, and Joe—nearly killed ourselves to open that business. Can you deny that Joe did more than his fair share?"

"No…" I admitted. "But that still doesn't make what you two did right." I took a deep breath. "You risked my money, Violet. *My money*. You should have consulted me."

"I didn't want to worry you."

"I'm not a child. You can't continue to treat me like one."

"I know you're not a child. That wasn't how I intended it. But you've been dealing with your breakup with Joe, then Daniel Crocker tracking you down… and Mason."

Something in the way she said his name caught my attention. "What about Mason?"

"The way Mason attacked Joe the other night scared me, Rose." She paused, then looked into my face, her eyes full of worry. "I've heard rumors and I'm worried about you."

"*What rumors?*"

Her mouth twisted. "I've said too much."

Had the truth of Mason's situation in Little Rock gotten out? "What rumors?"

"Just that he has a terrible temper." She grimaced. "A couple of days ago I noticed the bruise on your arm." She took my hand. "Is Mason hurting you, Rose?"

I jerked away from her, horrified. "No! Mason loves me. He would never hurt me."

"Then how did you get the bruise on your arm?"

There was no way I was going to admit that Mason had grabbed my arm during a nightmare about beating up his sister's killer. "It doesn't matter how I got it. That's not why I'm here. I'm here because you've sabotaged our business."

"Sabotaged?" Her voice rose, then she scowled and looked down the hall to see if she'd roused the kids. "I haven't sabotaged anything," she said in a hushed voice. "I freely admit that I was somewhat irresponsible with the finances—"

70

"*Somewhat?*"

"—but I meant well, Rose. You have to know that."

"Whether you meant well is beside the point, Violet. We nearly lost our business."

Her face lit up. "But we didn't! See? It all worked out!" She gave me a tiny frown. "Even if Mason refused to help."

"Mason didn't refuse to help. When I finally told him about the situation, he offered."

"*And you turned him down?* Who's the irresponsible one now, Rose?" She shook her head. "Again with your stupid pride."

"I was going to let him help," I answered, trying not to sound defensive. "But he would have needed to take the money out of his 401K and it wouldn't have gotten here in time."

"Why couldn't he just write you a check?"

"Most people don't have five or six thousand dollars just lying around." I shouldn't have admitted Mason didn't have the money, but I couldn't bear to hear her accuse Mason of not wanting to help. Or of me passively allowing our business to die.

"He's an attorney, Rose. What's he doin' with his money?"

"He works for the *county*. Ask Joe how much *he's* makin' now."

"Mason used to work for the DA's office in Little Rock. Joe told me he had to be makin' good money there. He was just as surprised as I was that Mason didn't step forward."

"And I'm sure he was more than happy to volunteer that information," I said sarcastically. "But that's not the point. The point is you got us into a terrible financial situation and didn't tell me about it until it was too late. Then you coerced my old boyfriend into helping us. We were supposed to be partners, Violet, but there's nothing going on here that suggests a partnership. In fact, you applied for that small business grant and never once told me you'd done so until I found out Joe's campaign stop was one of the strings attached."

"What do you mean we *were* supposed to be partners?"

"We might have saved the nursery, but I meant it when I said I quit."

Her eyes widened. "Rose, be reasonable."

I stood and began to pace. "I decided to split the business apart even before I found out about Joe."

She jumped to her feet. "You *what*?"

"I love you, Violet, but working together isn't going well. You have to know that."

"You're being utterly ridiculous."

"There you go again." I turned to face her. "Belittling me! Just because my opinion differs from yours, doesn't make it ridiculous."

Violet moved toward me cautiously, eyeing me like I was a rabid dog. "Okay, Rose. Calm down and we'll discuss your feelings."

I took a step backward. "We're not discussing my *feelings*. We're talking about the future of the Gardner Sisters Nursery."

"That's what I'm trying to do, but you're being irrational."

I took a deep breath. "If you want to discuss irrational behavior, how about we talk about Brody MacIntosh's wife vandalizing the store?"

Violet had the decency to look embarrassed.

"What is going on with you, Violet? A married man? I thought you were trying to work it out with Mike."

"You don't know anything about my life, Rose. Don't you stand there and judge me!"

"But he went back to his wife, and you're *still* sleeping with him!"

"I love him, Rose." She sat down on the sofa, tears streaming down her face. "I love him."

My heart softened, and I sat next to her, lowering my voice. "How did this happen?"

She shrugged, wiping her face. "How does any affair happen? The people involved usually feel unloved and unneeded by their spouse."

"But Mike—"

"Mike hasn't really loved me for a very long time."

"Are you sure?"

She released a tiny laugh, looking down the hall. "I think I'd know."

"I'm sorry." And I was. I couldn't imagine being married to someone who didn't love me.

"Yeah." The corners of her mouth lifted. "Me too." She turned to look at me. "I have nothing, Rose. You have Mason now, but I lost Brody. Especially after his wife…" Her voice trailed off. "I was desperate. That's why I turned to Joe. I need the nursery. You have to know that I would never purposely hurt you."

I used to think that. Now I wasn't so sure. "You still should have asked."

"I know. I'm sorry."

She was so quick to apologize that I couldn't help but wonder if she was following the philosophy that it was easier to ask for forgiveness than permission. "We still have to decide what to do with the business."

"There's nothing *to* do. Our problems are solved."

I shook my head. "It's far from fixed. I'm still planning to split the store from the landscaping business, but now I'm not sure what to do about Joe." I turned to her. "Did he really pay off the entire loan?"

"All one hundred and thirty-six thousand dollars of it."

I leaned back into the cushions and closed my eyes. "I'll never be able to repay that."

"Rose, he doesn't want you to. He wants to be part owner."

Opening my eyes, I shook my head. "That's never gonna work, Violet. Besides, his priorities are bound to change now that Hilary is here…and pregnant."

"He's not leaving Henryetta, whether he's with you or not, Rose. In fact, he's looking for a house to buy. Outside of the city limits."

I was neither surprised to hear that he was looking nor that Violet knew his plans. He was probably looking for something closer to me. "That was before Hilary showed up."

"He's not going to marry her."

"Whether he marries her or not is none of my concern now." Only it felt like it was. Thinking of Joe married to Hilary sent a fire of anger through my blood. But maybe Violet was right. Joe kept running back to her like a bad habit, but he didn't love her. And a baby wasn't a good enough reason to marry someone. Still, Hilary had a hold on Joe that defied logic.

Violet's eyes narrowed with determination. "Trust me. Joe's not goin' anywhere."

"Okay, let's say he's staying. Then the two of you can keep the storefront and Bruce Wayne and I will handle the landscaping portion."

"Bruce Wayne?" Her chin lowered as her eyes pierced mine. "You mean as your employee, right?"

I took a deep breath, preparing myself for another round of arguing. "No, Vi. Not as my employee. He'll be my partner."

"Where'd he get the money to buy in? Is he selling drugs?"

Her comment infuriated me. "He put up the same amount of money *you* did. Nothing."

She gasped.

"I don't expect you to understand my decision, nor do I expect you to approve. I'm simply telling you how I'm restructuring."

"Rose...Let's talk more about this."

I lifted my shoulders. "We have a lot of logistics to discuss about splitting the business, but we have nothing to discuss in regard to Bruce Wayne."

"Have you told Mason?" I heard the accusation in her voice.

"Yes, and he stands behind my decision if for no other reason than because it is *my* business and *my* decision."

"Rose." Her voice lowered. "Bruce Wayne's a stoner with a terrible reputation. What's that going to do for your business?"

"We haven't been hurtin' for jobs yet, and it's almost December. Not exactly peak planting time."

"But that was with him as an employee, not a co-owner. And how's it going to look if you jump into a business arrangement with a known criminal?"

If only she knew about my latest mess with Skeeter. "I don't care what the people in this town think."

She frowned her disapproval. "You should. You need them to like you or they'll never give you business."

"Again, we haven't been hurting."

"That's because I'm the face of the business."

My eyebrows rose. "I wouldn't be so sure about that after the mayor's wife is arrested for vandalism."

A sheepish grimace lifted the corner of her mouth. "I'm not going to press charges."

"What?"

She put her hand on my arm. "Calm down, Rose. The insurance will still pay, so what good would it do? She's sorry."

"*You've* talked to her?"

"No, but Joe did."

"And he approves of this?"

She nodded, tears brimming her eyes. "The town's still gonna talk, but things will die down sooner now."

I hated to admit that I saw the wisdom in that. What Brody's wife did was dead wrong, but pressing charges wasn't going to solve anything. "So what's gonna happen with you and Brody?"

"If Brody left her now, it would be more than scandalous. If he stays for a while, things will eventually blow over. The timing will be better."

I could tell how devastated she was. It was obvious that she really loved him. "Any chance she'll get back together with the Walmart manager from Lafayette County?"

She shook her head, looking more pathetic than I'd ever seen her. "He got transferred to Jonesboro. He ended it."

I sighed. What a mess. "I'm still splitting the business, Vi."

She grasped her hands on her lap. "I can't buy you out, Rose. You know that."

"I know, and despite calling you an employee earlier, I have no intention of taking the store from you." I looked at her. "I'm not sure how this is going to work exactly. I still need the nursery for the plants and trees. You've got all the accounts set up already, so it doesn't make sense to duplicate them. Maybe all the money will be dealt with under one big business, which will be under my control, and then you'll run the nursery and I'll run the landscaping portion."

She shook her head. "How's that any different than it is now?"

"You're losing financial control. You'll run the nursery and deal with the expansion, but anything involving budgeting needs my approval." I took a breath. "And I'm gonna have an accountant run the books."

"What?"

"I don't trust you, Violet, plain and simple. And I don't want to deal with it."

"That's too expensive. We couldn't make the loan payments."

"We don't need to worry about the loan payments anymore, do we? You sure took care of that." I gave her a wry smile. "We'll use the money that was supposed to go to the loan payments to pay the accountant."

"We'll have to get Joe's approval."

I shook my head. "Joe's not a partner. He has no say."

"Rose." Her eyes widened in frustration. "Joe bailed us out. He paid off the loan and paid for a few other things besides. You said yourself that you can't pay him back, and you've admitted on multiple occasions that we couldn't have gotten the nursery going without his help. Face it. He was a partial owner before we even opened."

I groaned. I was sure that Jonah was right and Joe had no legal claim on the business, but it did feel wrong to just take his money. "Maybe he'll let me set up a payment plan to reimburse him."

"No, he made it clear to me that he wanted to be a partial owner."

My anger flared again, but yelling at her wouldn't help anything. "I need to think about it. What has the insurance company said?"

"They say we can start cleanup next week. Joe walked through the shop and says it's not as bad as it looks. We have to replace the merchandise and some display shelves, but we shouldn't have any problems. Joe's going to front the money so we can get started right away and we'll use the insurance money to pay him back. We can open by the first of the year. In the meantime, we'll sell the Christmas trees from the lot."

I suppressed another groan. More involvement from Joe. "I'll need to speak to him about that. You're no longer involved in this discussion. And I'll need all the contact information for the insurance company so I can deal with them directly."

She started to protest, then stopped. "Okay."

My eyebrows lifted in surprise. No argument? "To be clear: we're doing nothing until I talk to Joe. And I suspect he'll be preoccupied for a while. In fact, he might be so preoccupied he'll decide he's not so eager to be a partner anymore."

"Or he might want the distraction."

Great. I suspected she was probably right. "Don't tell anyone that Joe's involved in this. At least for now."

"What are you going to tell Mason?"

What was I going to tell him? I couldn't imagine it going well.

Chapter Six

Bruce Wayne

I'd done screwed up big time.

The thing is, I knew it even as I was jumping into the middle of it. Kinda like when you're driving and you see a car about to rear-end you and there's not a doggone thing you can do to stop it from plowing into you. That's exactly how it was when Rose was dead-set on talking to Skeeter Malcolm.

In the few short months I'd worked for Rose Gardner, I'd learned one thing: Once she gets an idea in her head, there's little chance of dissuading her. And seeing how there was no way to talk her out of it, I helped her.

I knew what people were gonna say if word got out. They were gonna accuse me of dragging her into Henryetta's underbelly. They already thought the worst of me and I was okay with it as long as they didn't think the worst of her too.

People had always assumed the worst of me, for as long as I could remember. Russell, the man who gave me his last name, hated my guts because of the man who'd gotten my mother pregnant the night of her senior prom. While Russell might have forgiven my mom for giving her virginity to the bad boy in her class, he sure never seemed to have forgotten about it judging from the way he looked at me. To add piss to the pool water, I looked just like Clark Kent Williamson. And if Clark Kent Williamson was nothing but trouble, then the fruit of his loins was bound to be too.

I tried my best to be a good boy, but when you get in trouble for things you haven't even done, you start figuring if you're gonna get in trouble anyway, you might as well get a little fun out of it. Russell always complained that I never took responsibility for nothing, and I never denied it.

So nobody was more surprised than me that when Rose offered me partial ownership in the landscape business, I wanted it.

But while I might have been lazy, I wasn't entirely stupid. When people heard about Rose making me a co-owner, they'd say I'd somehow tricked her.

If anything, she'd tricked me.

I tried to turn down her offer, but she refused to let me help her with Skeeter unless I agreed. So I did. I had to, since I knew she'd seek him out on her own otherwise. Lettin' her do that would have been like puttin' a bunny in a cage with a wild dog.

Only it didn't turn out like I expected.

When Skeeter got angry, wanting to know how Rose knew about the robbers, I panicked and told him about Rose's visions. I didn't see any other way to help her at the time, but as soon as the words were out of my mouth, I realized my mistake. For one thing, Rose had no idea

I'd even figured out her secret. But more importantly, *Skeeter* knew her secret now, and a talent like Rose's was something he was going to keep in his back pocket.

Which meant that Rose was good and stuck.

But Rose didn't even seem to see the danger she was in. The very fact she kept back-talking Skeeter was proof enough of that. Sure, he thought it was cute, but it was like when some mouthy toddler didn't mind his parents. It might be funny at first, but the cuteness would soon wear off and all you were left with was annoyance.

The way the auction shook out hadn't sat well with me. When the sheriff showed up, I'd just about had a heart attack. Joe Simmons would have skinned Rose alive if he'd caught her, but he would have locked me up and made sure I had plenty of gray hair before I ever tasted freedom again. But Rose had surprised me. Not only had she gotten away, but she'd held her own and earned Skeeter's respect. For now. Something plenty of grown men had never done, myself included.

Now Fenton County was abuzz with gossip about the Lady in Black and I was fairly certain Rose was oblivious to it all. She thought she was done with Skeeter but I'd bet my right eye that she'd only just seen the beginning.

So now she had her money back, which meant the nursery was safe. Even though she'd said she would share it with me in exchange for helping her, I wasn't about to hold her to it. I'd learned desperate people would make all sorts of promises to get out of trouble.

Even so, Rose was different. I'd noticed that right away when she sat on my jury. While all the other jurors looked like they were about to pass out from the heat of the broken air conditioner, Rose watched the trial like it held the secret of life. Sure, she passed out, but I later realized it happened at the very moment she realized I was innocent. And when my old neighbor took the stand and told the judge that Rose had been snooping around Frank Mitchell's house, investigating my case, you could have knocked me over with a feather. Judge McClary threw her in jail for contempt of court, and I watched in disbelief as she was escorted out of the courtroom.

Why would someone I didn't even know risk so much to help *me*?

The very next week she sat across a table from me, both of us stuffed into a tiny room with my worthless attorney. She held her ground when my lawyer tried to make her look like a fool, and when she stared into my eyes, I about fell over. She truly believed I was innocent. Other than my best friend David, she was the only one who did. But truth be told, there were a few times when I'd seen doubt in David's eyes.

I spent plenty of sleepless nights pondering it. Why *did* she believe in me?

At first I wondered if she wanted something, but for the life of me, I couldn't figure out what it could be. After I was released, I waited for her to show up asking for favors, but she never did. Not for a couple months and then not for what I expected.

When David called to tell me that she wanted us to help her plant flowers at the new reverend's church, I thought he was high on 'shrooms. But he swore to me that he was at work and sober.

"*That's* what she wants from me?" I asked in disbelief.

David sounded leery. "So what do you wanna do?"

I hadn't worked since before my arrest for Frank Mitchell's murder. No one would hire me, so there was no denying that I needed the money. But I could have been rolling in a bed full of hundred-dollar bills and I still would have gone. I owed her. I figured I'd pay off my debt, collect my paycheck, and be done with her.

Little did I know I'd only just begun with her.

Little did I know I'd finally found my purpose in life.

One summer when I was twelve, my momma couldn't take the bickering between me and Russell anymore, so she packed me up and sent me to her uncle's farm. I mostly helped him with the cattle, but my aunt had a garden and I helped her weed the beds. Before the summer was over, she was calling me Farmer Bruce.

I planned to go back the following summer. Instead, I ended up doing my first stint in juvie for shoplifting.

Maybe it was working at a church. Maybe it was Reverend Jonah making me think I could do more with my life. Or maybe it was the woman who believed in me more than I believed in myself... Whatever the reason, when I first promised Rose I'd help her, it was because I owed her, but when I agreed to work with her on Jonah's house, I did it because I loved it.

Rose gave me my life back twice. And I wasn't about to forget that.

When I was in fourth grade, I read a book about a Chinese proverb. I wasn't much of a reader, but I had a book report due. I grabbed the book out of the school library, hardly looking at the cover—I just needed a book to skim so I could write the report. But later that night, I started reading it and couldn't put it down. It was about two men, a fisherman and a merchant. The merchant thought he was high and mighty and treated the fisherman like pond scum. The merchant needed to get to the other side of a lake in a hurry, so he asked the fisherman to use his boat to take him. Once they'd started their journey, the merchant confessed he couldn't swim, which the fisher found ridiculous. But halfway across the lake, a sudden storm blew in and tipped the boat over. The fisherman frantically searched the water and pulled the merchant from his almost watery grave, laying him on top of the overturned boat.

"Why did you save me?" the merchant asked. "I already paid you, and I didn't hide how disgusting I thought you were."

"Everyone deserves a second chance," the fisherman replied.

Once they got back to shore, the merchant swore his loyalty to the fisherman. He said he owed his life to him, and from them on, he would forever be in his debt.

For some reason that story stuck with me. Maybe it was because I could relate to the fisherman. Maybe it was because the merchant got his plate of humble pie—

something I wished could happen to the high-and-mighty people in my life. Or maybe I just wanted to think someone could change their mind about me. You see, I always saw myself as the fisherman until I met Rose Gardner and I realized I'd got the story all wrong. The fisherman knew who he was the whole time. And I didn't know who I was until I met Rose.

But she had saved me twice, so what could I possibly do to pay her back? To my mind, taking her to see Skeeter Malcolm had done twenty times more harm than good. Even if Rose didn't see it, I'd got her into the mess. Now I was gonna have to figure a way out of it.

The morning after Thanksgiving I sat around in my house, twiddling my thumbs. We were plumb outta jobs and Rose was planning to split up the business, which meant there wouldn't be anything to do for a while. But now that I'd had a taste of doing something I loved, I wasn't content to sit around. Rose owned the whole shebang—the store and the landscaping part—even if she planned to split it apart. Right now the store was in shambles and someone had to clean it up. I figured I'd head over after lunch and get a good look at what we were facing.

Rose's truck was in the parking lot when I pulled up to the store. I usually hated coming to the nursery, but only because Violet was always there, looking down her perky nose at me. But today her car was nowhere to be seen.

I found Rose inside the shop, sitting on a folding chair in a small area that had been cleared of debris, two other folding chairs arranged in front of her. "Rose?" I asked as walked through the door.

She turned to face me with a faraway look in her eyes, then gave me a soft smile. "What are *you* doin' here, Bruce Wayne? I gave you the day off, remember?"

"Sittin' around didn't feel right so I came to assess the damage. See what needed fixin'." I sat in one of the chairs in front of her. "What are *you* doin' here?"

"Trying to figure out the right thing to do."

I chuckled. "You know what it is. Sounds like you don't like it, but you know all the same."

She shook her head, her eyes sparkling with mischief. "Neely Kate better watch out. You're giving her a run for her money."

I wasn't sure what she meant by that, but it was good to see her more like herself. "I heard everyone in town got their money back. I'm guessin' you did too?"

"Who'd a thought Skeeter would be a man of his word?"

"Don't count on that bein' a regular occurrence. In fact, steer clear of him if you can."

She gave me an exasperated look. "It's not like I plan on paying him weekly visits for tea."

The thought of Skeeter drinking from a tea cup with his pinky sticking out nearly made me laugh, but there were more serious issues underfoot. "*You* might not be planning on visiting Skeeter, but you know *he's* gonna be calling on you. He's gonna want you to help him again."

Her lips pressed together. "No way. I can't."

"Skeeter's not used to hearin' no. He's got ways of makin' people do what he wants them to do."

"Mason's in his office right now with the DA and the sheriff and they're all abuzz about that woman with Skeeter." She turned to me with pleading eyes. "Mason's gonna kill me if he finds out who she really is. And what if the big-wigs in town learn that it was his girlfriend...he could lose his job because of me." She shook her head. "No. I can't risk doing anything like that again."

"And I'm telling you that you might have every intention of saying no, but you better have a plan in place for how to handle the situation when you say yes."

She released a frustrated sigh. "No sense borrowing trouble, Bruce Wayne. I'll cross that road when I come to it."

"You can't—"

"There's nothing I can do about it now, right?"

I hated to admit that she was right.

"Besides, there's plenty of other things we need to talk about. About the business."

My heart pounded in my chest. Had she changed her mind about making me a partner after all? It stung like a hornet in the ass, but I could hardly blame her. I decided to beat her to it. "I've been thinking." I looked down at the floor. "I'm not really the business owner type, you know? Maybe you shouldn't make me a partner, Miss Rose."

She was silent for several seconds, so I glanced up to look at her.

A fire lit behind her eyes before they narrowed on me. "What in tarnation are you talking about? We made a deal, Bruce Wayne Decker. Do I strike you as a reneger? Because I never considered you one."

I tried to keep from smiling. "No, ma'am. To both."

"And what's with this Miss Rose crap?"

I couldn't hold back my grin.

Her anger faded. "Bruce Wayne, as long as I own a nursery, you're gonna be a partner. Are we clear on that?"

"Yes, ma'am."

She sighed. "But I guess there's another partner in the mix."

I almost gasped in surprise. "*What?* Who?"

Her gaze leveled on me. "Joe."

Before I even thought about what I was doing, I groaned and stood. "You asked him to bail you out?"

"No!" she protested as she stood too. She moved behind the chair and gripped the back of it as though she needed help anchoring herself. "Violet convinced him to help us and neither one of them told me until after the fact." She paused. "He not only caught us up; he paid off the loan. Over one hundred and thirty thousand dollars, Bruce Wayne. I can't pay that back, not for a long time."

"You know he hates me, Rose. He's never gonna put up with me being a partner. But it's okay if you don't—"

Her eyes narrowed again. "I thought we just agreed to put that nonsense behind us."

"If he's a partner, he's never gonna agree."

"You let me worry about Joe Simmons. I still own the vast majority of the business. Right now, I'm trying to work through the logistics of it all. I want to let Joe and Violet have the storefront while you and me have the landscaping business. I've been sitting here trying to figure out how to make it work, and I think we'll need our own office. The less I deal with Violet, the better."

"Our own office?" I couldn't help smiling. "Does that mean I get a desk?" I teased.

"Do you want one?" She was serious.

I snorted. "What would I do with a desk?"

She shrugged. "Draw up landscaping plans. File all the paperwork for your clients. Use it as a place to keep your computer with landscaping software on it." Her eyebrows lifted. "Do you want me to go on?"

"You're serious?"

"Why wouldn't I be? I'm dreamin' big, Bruce Wayne. I need you to dream big with me." Her smile widened. "Can you do that?"

I nodded. I'd never dreamed big before, but I was willing to give it a try.

Chapter Seven

Rose

I wasn't looking forward to seeing Mason that evening. Not because I'd changed my mind about him. It was far more likely that he'd change his mind about me when he heard all the details I hadn't told him about the last two days.

It was nearly five when I finally went home. The smell of something delicious hit my nose as soon as I walked in the front door. I found Maeve peeling potatoes at the kitchen sink with Muffy lying at her feet.

"You didn't have to cook dinner, Maeve," I said as I walked over to the counter to check out the contents of the crockpot. "Although I can honestly say I don't think I've ever smelled anything so good in my life."

She flashed me a grin. "It's Italian Beef. Mason and Savannah loved it when they were kids, so I figured I'd make some for dinner. It's easy, so don't be worrying that I'm going to too much trouble."

"But you cooked almost the entire Thanksgiving dinner by yourself and now this," I said, looking into the glass lid. "I don't want you to think we invited you here just to cook for us."

"Speak for yourself," Mason teased, standing in the kitchen doorway. "I *always* hope she'll cook when she comes to visit."

My stomach cramped with anxiety, which was at war with my elation that he was home early. "Mason, what are you doing here?"

His grin widened and he walked over to me and wrapped an arm around my back, pulling me close. "Turns out I live here now."

"You lived here before, silly."

"Before it was temporary." His eyebrows lifted mischievously, and then he gave me a quick kiss. "Now it's more permanent."

"That's not what I meant and you know it." I patted his chest. "When I stopped by your office this afternoon you were up to your elbows in work. What changed so you could get loose?"

"My mother telling me she was leaving first thing tomorrow morning, for starters."

My mouth gaped. "What?" I turned to her. "You were supposed to stay until Sunday. I'm so sorry to have heaped so much work on you."

Maeve turned to me with a gentle smile. "Rose, calm down. I love cooking and helping you. And trust me, I don't do anything I don't want to do. Mason gets his hard-headedness from his mother, not his father."

"Mom," Mason grumbled good-naturedly. "Let Rose find out about my annoying traits on her own. Don't be helping her out."

"I already knew you were as stubborn as a pack mule, Mason Deveraux," I teased. "Shoot, half the county knows it."

Mason pulled me closer and lowered his mouth inches from mine. "And look how my stubbornness paid off. It got me you."

"I thought that was patience."

"Two sides of the same cloth."

I wondered how Maeve felt with Mason being so affectionate with me in front of her, but she beamed at the two of us. "I guess it's a good thing Mason's father wasn't as stubborn as him," I said. "Or you would have had your hands full."

"His father was quite a pushover, actually. Savannah was just like *him*."

Something in Maeve's words sobered Mason and he stiffened slightly. "Yes, she was."

Alarm flickered in Maeve's eyes. "In any case, I'm going home a day early to start packing up my house. My offer was accepted and closing is even sooner than I anticipated. I'd like to get all settled in by Christmas."

"Do you want me to come with you and help?" I asked. I hated to think of her packing up her entire house on her own. "That's a massive undertaking."

She flashed me a smile. "You just went through your own move. I couldn't put you through that twice in such a short period of time. Besides, I think you're needed in Henryetta right now. You still have your business to sort out after the vandalism and all."

Mason leaned back. "Did you get the loan taken care of?" he asked me. "Did you have some kind of problem with it that you couldn't discuss at the courthouse?"

I cast a glance at Maeve. "I should help your mom with dinner."

She waved a hand. "You two go talk about Rose's business. I'll finish up here."

"Oh, I couldn't—"

"Go."

With no excuses left, I released a huge breath. "Let's go into the office."

Mason hobbled behind me as I walked into the office like a prisoner on death row and sat on the edge of the desk.

"Now you have me worried, Rose," Mason said, watching me closely as he shut the French door behind him. "Why don't you want to talk about the loan?"

"Not for the reasons you probably think."

"Then why don't you tell me and I'll tell you if I'm off."

"You should sit down." I gestured to one of two leather chairs in front of the desk. "You've been on your feet too much today. I can tell by the way you're moving so slow, not to mention I saw you standing when I dropped by your office."

He sat in the chair with a grim expression. "Why are you stalling?"

I took a deep breath, clasping my hands in my lap. "I didn't pay off the loan."

Horror crossed over his face. "What happened? Did you lose the business?"

I shook my head, feeling sick to my stomach. "No. The loan had already been paid off before I got a chance to make the payment."

Confusion flickered in his eyes. "I don't understand. How did it get paid off? Violet doesn't have that kind of money."

"No, she doesn't," I said slowly. "But she knows someone who does."

He stared blankly at me for several seconds before his eyes filled with fury. "*Goddamn him!*"

I guessed he'd figured out who it was. "Mason, your mother's in the kitchen."

He jumped to his feet. "I don't care if Gandhi's in the kitchen!" His voice boomed in the office. "Who the hell does Joe Simmons think he is?"

"I honestly think he was trying to help."

"*You're defending him?*"

I put my hand on his arm. "Mason, will you just hear me out?"

His face hardened. "It's your business, Rose. You can do whatever you like."

Tears filled my eyes. "Mason, don't be like this."

"Like what? Outraged that your ex-boyfriend is manipulating you in an attempt to win you back? Or that you're actually falling for it?"

I put my hands on my hips, furious. "Are you calling me *stupid*, Mason Deveraux?"

Defeat washed over his face. "No, Rose. You are far from stupid. In fact, I don't think you give your intelligence enough credit." He moved closer to me. "But you are by far one of the kindest souls I've ever met, and unfortunately some people in this world will try to use that to their own advantage and hurt you in the process." He wrapped his arms around my back and tugged me to his chest, lifting me off the desk. "I'm sorry for my temper. Why don't you tell me what happened and I promise to not fly off the handle this time."

"Okay," I said, still feeling hurt, but I wasn't sure why. If the roles were reversed and some old girlfriend of Mason's gave him a bunch of money when I couldn't, I doubt I'd be very gracious about it. I moved back to the edge of the desk and tugged him toward the chair. "But there's not much to tell. I told you that Violet wanted to meet me at eleven, but Joe was with her. Violet had told him about our money troubles and he'd offered to help. Only neither one bothered to discuss it with me until this morning. By then the deed had been done. But Joe didn't just cover the overdue loan payments, he paid off the loan in its entirety."

"How much was the loan?"

I swallowed, feeling sick again. "About one hundred and thirty-six thousand dollars."

Mason's face paled. "You're kidding."

"I wish to God I was."

I could see from the expression on his face that he was calculating numbers, so I wasn't surprised when he said, "After my loan for my condo is paid off, there's not much left of my settlement. But if I cash in my 401K like I mentioned, we can pay him off. Barely."

I shook my head. "I can't let you do that."

"Rose, we're a couple now. I want to help you."

"We're brand new, Mason. That's too much of a commitment."

"Yesterday we thought we were having a baby together. You can't get much of a bigger commitment than that."

He was right, but I still couldn't take his money.

His gaze shifted to the paperwork on his desk before returning to my face. "You didn't know about any of this until after the fact, which means you didn't sign any paperwork, right?" He looked more hopeful. "You didn't sign anything this morning, did you?"

"No."

He scowled. "I'd ask you how he got the loan number, but it's Henryetta and he probably got it from Violet. Even without her, Mr. Burns is probably so eager to recoup money from the loans Norman Sullivan gave out, he probably didn't bat an eye about letting Joe pay off your note."

"I know what you're getting at, Mason. That Joe may have sunk money into the business, but he doesn't have the right to lay claim to any of it."

He nodded. "Exactly. He may have paid off the loan, but he did so of his own free will. You owe him nothing, Rose."

I didn't say anything.

"But it's not in you to let him pour that much money into your business without having any say. Is it?"

Tears filled my eyes. "I'm sorry."

"Let me pay him back, sweetheart."

"I can't."

I could see he was getting angry again, but he was struggling not to yell, which made him sound distant instead. "Then tell me why you'll take *his* money and not mine."

"For one, I'm certain he can afford it. That much money's nothing to the Simmons family. But Violet was also right when she told me that Joe was already like a partial owner before the nursery opened. He put a lot of work into helping us get it going. Sure, I think part of the reason he gave us the money was to try to get me back, but I also think part of it was because he really doesn't want our business to fail."

Mason shook his head, his face reddening. "Do you know how many alarm bells your explanation just set off? Do you really want to take the Simmonses' money?"

I didn't say anything. Mason gently took my hand between both of his own. "I love you, Rose, and I'm scared."

His statement caught me by surprise. "Why would you be scared?"

"I'm scared of losing you." He heaved a sigh. "Last weekend you admitted to kissing Joe after he forced himself on you and now he's rushed in like a white knight to save your business."

"Mason, I love you. I want to be with *you*." I understood his fear but I wasn't sure what else to do to reassure him. But then I knew. "If Joe instigated this to get me back, you don't have to worry about that anymore. He's going to have his hands full. In fact, I suspect there's a good chance he might leave town."

Mason's head tilted. "Why would he do that?"

"After Joe and Violet informed me about the loan, I told them both I quit—"

"Wait. You didn't tell me that."

"That's because nothing came of it. As soon as I quit, Hilary showed up at the nursery."

"Hilary? Is J.R. trying to get Joe to go back into the political ring?"

"I'm sure it's his end goal, but that wasn't why she was there." I paused. "Hilary is pregnant. And I don't think she's lying. She set up an ultrasound for this afternoon so Joe could see the baby for himself. There's no way she could fake that."

Mason's eyes widened and he sat back in his chair.

"Mason? What's wrong?" I thought my news would have reassured him, but he wasn't looking reassured.

He stood and pulled me off the desk. "Rose, I know we're still fairly new together, but I've loved you for months. You're the most important thing in my life. You know that, don't you?"

"Why are you telling me this?"

He gently kissed me, then gave me a soft smile. "If you want to be with Joe, then I want you to be with him. I don't want to be your second choice."

"You're not, Mason. I swear. Why are you telling me this?" I asked again, starting to panic.

"The Gardner Sisters Nursery is *your* business, Rose. I'll support you in any way I can—from manual labor to drawing up the paperwork to officially make Bruce Wayne your co-owner for the landscaping portion. My money—both the settlement check and my 401K—is yours if you want it. But if you don't, I'll stand by your decision."

I stared at him in disbelief. "Why would you do that if you don't agree?"

"Because I can't force you to do what I want. Part of the reason I love you is that you aren't afraid of what people might say or think, so I wouldn't try to take that away from you. All I ask is that you let me help you in some way so I feel like I'm part of your business too."

"Oh, Mason." I threw my arms around his neck and buried my face into his chest. "Thank you."

Mason was quiet all through dinner, but as we were starting to clear off the kitchen table, he pulled his phone out of his pocket and grimaced. "I have to go into the office."

"Is everything okay?" I asked as he grabbed his coat and headed for the front door.

"It will be."

Chapter Eight

Joe

I pulled up in front of the Henryetta Family Clinic at four fifty-five, although I wasn't sure why I was there. If Hilary had actually made the damned ultrasound appointment, I knew she wasn't bluffing. But if she was pregnant with my kid, going to see one of those fuzzy black-and-white images was what I was supposed to do, right?

I'd been on autopilot ever since she dropped her grenade, screwing up any hope I had of winning back Rose. I would never be able to wipe the image of Rose's horrified face from my memory. She'd had a vision of me winning a U.S. Senate race with a very pregnant Hilary at my side. I hadn't believed her. In fact I'd sworn to her that it could never happen, but look where I was now—about to see my baby for the first time.

My baby was supposed to be with Rose.

Yesterday, I thought Rose was pregnant with Mason's baby. Today, Hilary was pregnant with mine.

It was amazing how quickly things had gotten turned on their head.

Hilary's Lexus was in the lot, so I got out of my sheriff's car and headed into the clinic. She sat waiting in one of the worn chairs in the waiting room, looking as fresh and pulled together as always. For a second I considered that she might be lying. Neely Kate was pregnant, and she was puking all over the place—including straight down Toby Wheaton's back at Jasper's, which he'd grumbled about when I questioned him. Neely Kate, who'd always prided herself on her appearance, looked like she was three days into a backpack camping trip most days lately. Hilary looked like she'd stepped off the cover of *Vogue*.

"Joe." She stood and met me in the center of the waiting room with a kiss on the cheek. "How was your afternoon?"

"Cut the bullshit, Hilary. I'm here to see the proof of my indiscretion. Let's not make it something it's not."

She gave me a patient smile, one with which I was all too familiar. It meant she considered my behavior to be that of a petulant child and she'd wait me out.

Mason Deveraux wasn't the only patient person I knew.

"Joseph. Language. There are children here."

I cast a glance at a toddler clinging to a waiting room chair while his mother studied her smart phone. "I think we're good."

The waiting room door opened and a woman in pink scrubs stood in the doorway. "Ms. Wilder, we can see you now."

I followed Hilary through the door and down a hall to an exam room, the nurse following behind us. "I'm Gina, the tech who will be performing your exam. Since you're wearing a dress, you'll need to disrobe and put on the gown that's on the exam table. You can leave on your bra, but be sure to remove your panties. I'll be back to check on you and your husband in a few minutes."

I started to cough.

"Are you okay, Mr. Wilder?" the nurse asked.

"That's Deputy Simmons," I corrected, more short than I'd intended. I rubbed my eyes. "I'm sorry, Gina. Please forgive my rude behavior." I flashed her a smile. "It's been a crazy twenty-four hours at work. I'm running on a few hours of sleep." Most of my sleeplessness was over Rose's possible pregnancy, but she didn't need to know that. "Hilary and I aren't married. We're not even a couple."

"Oh." Gina's eyes widened and I could feel Hilary's daggers of hate bounce off my back.

"In fact, I'm the new chief deputy sheriff in town and I've only lived here a few weeks. What do single people do in Fenton County?"

Gina's cheeks blushed and I felt bad about leading her on, but it was worth the discomfort Hilary was going through. I could tell she was furious by the low *hmm* in her throat.

"There's a single's group at the new church—The New Living Hope Revival Church. It's run by—"

"Jonah Pruitt," I finished, guilt mixing with my anger. That man was the very reason I was in this situation.

"So you've heard of him? He has a TV show and everything."

"I've heard of him."

Gina left the room and Hilary grinned at me, looking like the Cheshire cat. "Jonah Pruitt..." she purred. "Isn't he the man Rose slept with after you went on the campaign trail?"

"They didn't sleep together. My father had it wrong."

"Really?" she asked as she reached around and unzipped her dress, letting it drop to her waist so I was staring at her expensive, lacy pink bra. "He rarely gets things wrong."

"Could you give me a little warning?" I asked, turning my back to her.

"It's nothing you haven't seen before."

"Oh, really? The breasts looked new."

She laughed, a dainty sound I was sure she'd spent hours perfecting. "You've always loved my breasts, Joe."

"I used to love ketchup on my mashed potatoes when I was in preschool," I said, staring at the wall. "But I outgrew it."

Hilary laughed again. "You can turn around now."

She was sitting on the exam table, the gown wrapped around her front.

"How far along are you?"

She shifted on the table, keeping her eyes on me. "Six weeks."

I did the math in my head.

"It's yours, Joe. You start figuring the gestation from my last period, so the timing still makes it yours." She paused. "Not that I slept with anyone else while you've sowed your wild oats."

I didn't answer. There was nothing to say.

The door opened and Gina walked in. "Are you ready to see your baby?"

"I'm already under a doctor's care in Little Rock," Hilary said, "but I wanted Joe to meet his baby too."

Gina's smile faded. "Oh."

I stood to the side of the exam table, resisting the urge to tell her to hurry it along. Spending this much time with Hilary was making my skin crawl.

Gina grabbed a wand with an attached cord and slathered it in a gel. "I'm just going to insert this into your vagina—"

My eyes widened. "What?"

"It's the best way to see everything," Gina volunteered, keeping her eyes on Hilary.

Hilary flashed me her patient smile.

I just wanted this nightmare to end.

Within a minute, a black, white, and gray blob appeared on the screen.

"There he is, Joe," Hilary said, pointing her finger toward the screen. "There's our boy."

"That blob?" I asked, turning to Gina. "You can tell it's a boy?"

"No," she said, looking at the screen. "It's much too early."

"I want Joe to see his heartbeat."

Gina moved the wand around for a good thirty seconds.

Hilary pushed up on her elbows, fear in her eyes. "Where's the baby's heartbeat?"

"I'm having trouble finding it." Gina gave her a tight smile. "The date of your last period puts you at six weeks and two days. It's still a bit early yet."

"No." Hilary sounded panicked. "My doctor found it on Wednesday."

Gina looked slightly concerned.

I glanced at Hilary, who was close to tears. I put my hand on her shoulder and gently pushed her back. "Hil, let the tech do her job. I'm sure you moving around isn't helping things. If the doctor found it on Wednesday, I'm sure everything is fine."

Hilary shook her head, her eyes wild. "No. I had some bleeding two weeks ago. It's early enough that there could have been a heartbeat on Wednesday and if there's not one now the baby could have died."

"Is that true?" I asked Gina in surprise.

"It happens more often than you think. A lot of times the mother never even realizes she's pregnant and thinks her period's late," she murmured. "Ah…here we go."

The black blob on the screen had a gray-pulsing spot. "That's *it*?" I asked.

"That's it." Gina sounded relieved.

I tried to wrap my head around the fact that the blob on the screen was a baby—my baby—but I felt nothing but an overwhelming sadness. How I wished it was Rose on that table with my baby and not the witch who had done everything in her power to ruin my life.

"How big is it?" I asked.

"Teeny-tiny," Gina said. "About the size of a pea." She turned to Hilary. "I took some measurements as if this were a regular appointment, especially since you said you had bleeding." She turned off the machine and removed the wand. "You can get dressed now."

Gina left the room and Hilary got dressed without comment while I stared at drawings of fetuses at various stages of development on the wall.

Hilary laid the gown on the table. "Thanks for coming, Joe," she said without her usual theatrics.

"If it's my baby, I suppose I should be here."

"It's yours," she said softly.

"I know." She had spent nearly every minute with me for weeks until I left her and the campaign to go save Rose from Daniel Crocker. I had to be the father. "I need some time to wrap my head around this, Hilary."

"I know."

Her complacency pissed me off. "You and my father set me up."

"I never forced you to sleep with me, Joe."

"But you sure waited until I was good and drunk to get the ball rolling."

"That wasn't too hard considering you were spending most of the time drunk. I'm worried the baby will have some type of birth defect."

"You should have considered that before you had unprotected sex with me."

"You never asked about birth control," she countered.

"You've been on the pill since we were seventeen. Why would I?"

"I don't want to fight with you, Joe."

"And what did you think was going to happen when I found out that you pulled the oldest trick in the book on me?" I shook my head with a sneer. "Really, Hilary. I expected something much more original from you."

"I need to go lie down." She picked up her purse and reached for the doorknob. "I'm staying at the B&B on Oak Street, close to downtown."

"You're staying in Henryetta? For how long?"

"I haven't decided yet."

Great. But I kept that to myself. I was tired of fighting her. What was done was done.

Hilary opened the door and started to walk through, then stopped and turned around. "She's moved on without you."

"What?"

"Rose. She's moved on without you. She's with the ADA now and she seems happy, don't you think?"

I closed my eyes and sighed. "I can't do this right now."

"I'll call you tomorrow."

I waited a couple of minutes to make sure she was really gone before I headed to the waiting room.

"Deputy Simmons," Gina called after me. "I forgot to give you this."

I spun around and she handed me a small image of the ultrasound.

"Your baby's first picture."

I stared at the blob. It looked more like a slug than a baby. "Thanks."

I was off for the night, so I picked up an order of hot wings from Big Bill's and a six-pack of beer. The tiny house I lived in while I was undercover didn't feel right without Rose. I needed to move, but I hated to leave Ashley and Mikey. Despite what Rose thought, I truly loved those kids. They were the one bright spot of coming back here.

No, my job was the biggest bright spot.

I'd moved back to be close to Rose, but I liked the challenge of turning the sheriff's department around after the corruption brought into it by my predecessor. Unlike my position with the state police, my dad had nothing to do with this job. It was all mine and it gave me a sense of pride, something with which I was fairly unfamiliar. The last time I'd felt pride was when I helped Rose and Violet set up the nursery. Violet had known exactly what she was doing when she let it 'slip' that the nursery was in dire straits. I jumped at the chance to help, even though I knew I was getting played. I went along with it first for Rose. She'd sunk her inheritance into the venture and she loved it. So, yes, part of the reason I made the investment is that I hoped to win her back. But I also felt a personal involvement in the Gardner Sisters Nursery. Now, though, everything had changed...

I picked up the photo of the ultrasound, trying to figure out how that splotch could be a baby. How would Hilary and I handle this? I refused to marry her. I didn't love her and I'd endured my parents' loveless marriage my entire life. I'd never do that to my kid. But while we might not get married, we still had to figure out how to raise a baby together.

The doorbell rang and I glanced at the time on my phone. It was almost eight o'clock. Hilary had lasted an hour longer than I'd expected. I opened the front door, surprised to see Mason Deveraux on my front porch.

I groaned. "What the hell do you want, Deveraux? Because I've had one hell of a day."

"So I've heard."

He'd used that same smug tone nearly a year ago when he'd ordered me to leave his sister alone. Some nights I lay awake, reliving that conversation, wishing I'd listened to him.

"Are you here to hit me? Because I'm hitting back this time."

Anger flashed in his eyes. "I want you to leave Rose alone."

"Rose is a grown woman, capable of making her own decisions."

"You and I both know what you're doing. If you care about her at all, you'll stop making her life difficult."

"She doesn't love you, Deveraux," I spit out. "You're her rebound until she's ready to take me back."

"You've got your own baggage to take care of, Simmons. I heard your fiancée is pregnant."

"She was never my fiancée."

"Someone needs to inform the press who wrote all that coverage about your upcoming nuptials."

I stepped out onto the porch, leaving the door open behind me. Deveraux was gunning for a fight and I was in the mood to give it to him. "You know all about press coverage, don't you?" I asked. "Whatever happened to the man you put into a coma?"

"The man who killed my sister?" he shouted. "I sure as hell didn't see you doing anything to avenge her death."

"Forgive me for leaving the matter to the wheels of justice."

"You made goddamn sure the wheels of justice didn't do a thing to help save her!" Mason shouted, grabbing my shirt in his left fist.

He was right. We both knew it, but his self-righteous attitude was pushing me over the edge. "At least I've never killed a man outside of the line of duty!"

Mason shoved me against the side of the house, still clutching my shirt. "You know what you did to Savannah, you low-life piece of shit. How do you live with yourself?"

"I used to live with myself just fine until you stole the woman I love." I shoved him away from me and he stumbled with his leg brace. "I know what you're doing, Deveraux. I know you've taken her to get back at me."

His eyes widened. "Are you insane? Has it even once occurred to you that I actually *love* her? Only I love her for her. You spent half your time with Rose trying to change her."

"Somebody needs to protect her, *you son-of-a-bitch*." I gave him a hard shove and he stumbled on his injured leg again, his back slamming into a support post on the porch. "If anything happens to her, I'm coming for you. I'll make sure you wish you'd never met her."

"Where was this protective streak when that man was stalking Savannah?"

"I never loved Savannah!" I shouted.

"But you sure didn't have any trouble sleeping with her."

"I hate to break it to you, Deveraux, but you don't need to love a woman to screw her."

He threw a punch, but I was prepared for it this time and I ducked, throwing one of my own and connecting with his upper lip.

He got in a jab to my stomach, knocking the breath out of me as I scrambled backward.

"Just like you keep screwing Hilary Wilder? All while declaring your love for Rose?" He sneered, wiping the blood off his lip with the back of his hand. "How many babies have you fathered across Arkansas, Simmons?"

"One! I've made damned sure of it."

His eyes hardened. "Are you sure about that?"

He uttered the question like a man holding a full house in a poker game. What did he know that I didn't? Oh God. Rose.

"Is Rose pregnant with my baby?" I choked out. "She said she wasn't pregnant."

My question enraged him. "*Rose*? No, thank God for her and that poor unfortunate child if she had been. Having to endure *your family*?" He threw another punch, clipping my eyebrow this time. "Not Rose, you worthless piece of shit! *Savannah*!"

My blood turned to sludge. "What?"

Tears filled his eyes and some of his anger faded. "Savannah was four and a half months pregnant when she was murdered, Joe. She wasn't the only one to die that night. Your baby died too." He choked on a sob. "The autopsy report said it was a girl."

I shook my head, feeling like I was going to pass out. "No. *No*! I would have heard about it in the news! There's no way something like that wouldn't be plastered everywhere!"

"We both know someone who had the power to cover that up," Mason growled, his hatred returning. "Someone who manipulates people's lives just for the fun of it."

My father.

Chapter Nine

I'd never hated anyone like I hated Joe Simmons.

Little Prince Simmons had spent his entire life screwing people and getting away with it. He'd make a mess and his daddy would send in a cleanup crew to tidy it up. He'd never accepted full responsibility for anything he'd done, Savannah included.

I'd known Joe Simmons by reputation before he even met my sister. It was hard to understand why he was hired by the state police in the first place, but I believed the rumors that Daddy Simmons had a hand in that as well. Joe was brash, reckless, arrogant. He was known as a loose cannon. But while he flouted the rules, he was known for his high success rate closing his cases.

I detested the man for that alone.

He flew in the face of everything I believed in: hard work, consequences, and justice. Of course, it was because he was my polar opposite my sister was as drawn to him as a fly to honey.

Savannah had been very close to our father, so when he died her sophomore year in high school, she didn't take it well. Within six months of his death she began to act out—she missed curfews and came home drunk. Her grades plummeted.

My mother was caught up in her own grief. Anyone who'd ever met my parents knew that theirs was a once-in-a-lifetime love. Mom tried to pull herself together for our sake, but she was rudderless without my father. And truth be told, I think part of her felt deserted by the man who had promised to love her forever.

I loved my father too. I'd never met a greater man—either personally or professionally. I was finishing my sophomore year of college at Duke when it happened. I took his loss just as hard as my mother and my sister, but I didn't have the luxury of being able to dwell on it. For all of my father's positive traits, he was terrible with money. He was a partner in a law firm, so his estate should have been enough to support my family, but he'd mismanaged his investments and let his life insurance policy lapse. Add on to that the falling markets had wiped out over half of his retirement savings, and we were left with very little. Though we weren't destitute, we had to change the way we lived.

Savannah saw my father's death as a betrayal of their close relationship, and the fact that he'd left us struggling financially was the straw that pushed her over the edge.

Mom was at a loss, and I was hundreds of miles away. I suggested Mom put her in counseling, but she was hesitant because of the money and the stigma. But Savannah was getting more and more out of control in her junior year, and her private high school was less lenient now that our usual donation of fundraising money had slowed to a trickle.

The summer between my junior and senior year, I was offered the chance to work in a friend's father's law firm in Nashville. But my family was imploding. I had to put their needs above my own, so I turned it down and returned home to work at an office supplies store.

Savannah and I clashed the second night I was home.

I was reading in the living room when she passed through. She was about to head out the door wearing a dress that was too tight and short, with enough eye makeup to risk being mistaken for a hooker.

"Are you going to a costume party?" I asked. "Because that's the only explanation I can come up with for why you look like a prostitute."

Savannah gasped in shock.

Mom, who was in the kitchen, stepped into the doorway. "Mason!"

I stood and moved toward my sister. "Do you have any idea how you look?"

She gave me a sneer that was probably supposed to look worldly, but it came across as the very opposite. "Guys like it."

I lifted my eyebrows. "I'm sure they do. But those aren't the type of guys you want, Savannah."

"What the hell do you know about what I want, Mason? You're never here! You don't know what we've been going through! You left us, just like he did!"

"Left you? Is that what you think I did?" I asked, my pain leaking through my words. "You know how much I hate being this far from you and Mom, especially now."

"Then come home, Mason," she begged, tears making thick lines of mascara run down her cheeks. "We need you."

Her request was a stab in my heart. She was right. They did need me, and the fact that she had pulled an abrupt change from her behavior moments ago only drove the knife deeper.

"We all have our places in this world," Mom said, stepping into the room. "Mason's place right now is at Duke, finishing his degree. It's what Dad would have wanted."

Savannah's lip curled in disgust. "Well Dad's not here, so screw him." And with that, she burst out of the front door, slamming it behind her.

Part of me wondered if I should follow after her, but I'd already handled the entire incident badly. Anything else I did that night was bound to just make it worse. "She's right," is all I said. "I should come back."

Mom sighed. "Are we going to discuss this *again*?"

We'd played out this conversation countless times. Me suggesting I come home and go to the university in Little Rock, Mom insisting against it.

"Your father went to Duke. He was so proud that you were following in his footsteps. You're about to start your final year, Mason. You'd have to repeat too many classes. You need to stay."

"You need me. Savannah needs me."

"I need you to finish what you set out to do. We'll make do. I promise."

I spent the next week observing Savannah and her friends. She clung to her boyfriend like a vine to a tree, and it was obvious that she was trying to make up for the loss of our father by attaching herself to a boy, but I was at a loss as to what to do about it. I'd tried talking to her twice—both times with far less hostility—but she wouldn't listen.

"We need to get away," I said one night a few weeks later after she'd left to meet some friends. I'd pushed Mom to set more boundaries with her, so she'd started to dress more conservatively, but I knew she was drinking and smoking pot. I smelled it on her every time she came home at two or three in the morning.

"You don't have to wait up for me," she'd say almost every time she came home.

"I know," I'd say in response. Of course, I still would. Each time she went out, I'd set up a vigil on the couch.

My mom's eyes widened at my suggestion.

"Mom, she's about to start her senior year in high school. She has to pull herself together or she's going to screw up her future."

"I know," she said, but I heard the defeat in her voice.

"How about we go to Uncle Ted's lake house up in the Ozarks for a couple of weeks?"

"The *cabin*?" Mom asked in surprise. "You used to hate it. Why would you want to go there?"

I grinned. "I was thirteen. I hated it because I couldn't play video games there. Savannah loved it."

A soft smile lit up her face. "She loved paddling the canoe around the cove." Her smile fell. "But she's not nine years old anymore, Mason. Her priorities have changed just like yours did. A canoe ride isn't going to entice her to go."

"With all due respect, Mom, she's a minor and you're the parent. You're in charge. You need to tell her that we're going, not give her the option."

"You're right." She looked hurt. "Your father was the disciplinarian."

I wasn't so sure that was true, especially in regard to Savannah. She'd had him wrapped around her pinky finger. But I'd followed the straight-and-narrow path, so other than a few adolescent transgressions, my parents hadn't needed to exercise their disciplinary skills much. But I didn't see how pointing that out would help anything. "But Dad's gone now, and Savannah needs you to be stricter."

"It's just that she's been through so much…"

"Let's just go away for a bit and see if we can get her to see reason."

"Okay."

Savannah didn't take the news too well, screaming and crying, shouting that I had single-handedly ruined her life.

My boss at the supplies store took it slightly less well, saying that if I left for two weeks I shouldn't bother coming back.

Mom's boss—my father's partner in the law firm—was much more agreeable. He'd hired her to help out at the law firm after becoming aware of our financial situation. I couldn't help but wonder if he had partially done it to save face: It was bound to reflect badly on an estate planning law firm if one of the former partners left his family financially bereft. The evidence for my supposition was the fact that my mother had a floating job that she could take off from at a moment's notice. Not that I'd ever point it out to her. She seemed to love the job, especially when she was asked to talk to the newly bereaved families who walked in lost and forlorn.

My mother was a collector of lost souls. Only she was too close to the lost soul in her own home to know what to do.

***

Uncle Ted hadn't been to the cabin in years and the neglect was apparent as we pulled into the drive. The front steps creaked under our weight and the bushes were overgrown. Part of the kitchen floor sagged from a leak in the roof and some rodent had made a nest behind the refrigerator, leaving a terrible smell. Savannah complained bitterly and I could tell my mother was beginning to second-guess our decision.

"So it needs a little TLC," I said. "It'll be fine after we clean it up."

"You're deluded," Savannah said in her most icy tone.

We just needed to give it a few days and things would get better, I just knew it.

123

But ten days into our fourteen-day stay, things still hadn't improved. If anything, they'd gotten worse. Savannah had moved past petulant to hostile and my mother was constantly in tears.

"This isn't helping, Mason," my mother said one night. "Maybe we should just go home."

"No." I was too stubborn to admit defeat. I'd given up two jobs this summer for Savannah—one of them a position most pre-law students would throw their best friend under the bus to get. I wasn't about to give up now. "I was thinking about going on a hike tomorrow. I'll take Savannah with me."

"She'll hate that."

"Too bad. I'm taking her anyway."

Truth be told, I was bored to tears at the lake house. I was used to being on the go, constantly working on something, and all the down time was making me anxious. I needed the hike. Bringing Savannah was an afterthought.

Mom was right. Savannah flipped out the next morning when I told her she was going with me. "You can't make me!" she screamed at the top of her lungs. "You're not the boss of me!"

Even with all of Savannah's theatrics, it wasn't hard to see that her outburst was motivated by a deep hurt. "Savannah, if you come with me on this hike, we can go home tomorrow," I said, more worried about her than ever. "Two days early."

That caught her attention. "Is this some kind of trick?"

"No. I swear. And you know I don't swear lightly."

A grin started to lift the corners of her mouth, but it disappeared almost before it began, as though she'd realized she was about to shift out of her character as the sour teenage girl. "You don't swear at all. You say promises are too easily broken."

"While you swear to everything and then renege on it all."

A real smile broke loose and then faded. It was a familiar childhood spat, rehashed a million different ways, but the fact that she'd instigated it renewed my hope that I could get through to her.

"Okay," she said. "But I don't want to get sweaty and dirty."

"But getting sweaty and dirty are the best parts," I teased.

Mom's eyes filled with tears as Savannah went to grab her backpack. "Thank you, Mason. That exchange was the first glimpse of our Savannah that I've seen in months."

"Don't thank me yet," I muttered as Savannah entered the kitchen. I'd traded away two days in exchange for one afternoon. I wasn't so sure it was a good barter.

We packed bottled water and protein bars and got in my car to drive the short distance to the trailhead. We hiked in silence for the first ten minutes, but it wasn't filled with the usual hostile tension that rolled off my sister. The silence was more tentative, as though she was open to accepting my help. But I was terrified. Each time

I'd tried to talk reason into her before, I'd only made matters worse. Maybe that was my problem. I needed to stop lecturing her.

About an hour into the hike, we stopped at the edge of a small bluff overlooking the lake. "Let's take a short break and enjoy the view for a minute," I said, pulling out my water bottle and sitting on a large rock.

"We *have* a view at that shack you're making us sleep in. Let's just get this hike over with so I can go home."

"Okay, *I'm* tired and need a break."

"Perfect Mason needs a break?" she asked, a razor in her voice.

"Is that what you think?" I asked without recrimination. "You think I'm perfect?"

She spun around, ready for battle. "Well, aren't you? *Mason graduated with a 4.2 GPA,*" she sing-songed. "*Mason got nearly perfect scores on his PSA. Mason never caused any trouble in high school.* How the hell am I supposed to live up to that?"

"Savannah, I'm far from perfect. And I caused plenty of trouble in high school." I grinned at her. "I just hung around with kids who were smart and sneaky enough not to get caught." I tossed her a protein bar, which she caught with two hands. "You just need to find new friends."

Her mouth dropped open, then her eyes narrowed. "What are you up to?"

I shrugged. "Nothing. I'm just tired of fighting with you. If you want to cause hell, more power to you. But find a group that's gonna do it right. The fun part of causing trouble is getting away with it. You get caught almost every time."

She relaxed a little, opening the protein bar package. "You're lying. I don't believe you ever caused any trouble."

"Goes to show how much you know me," I laughed and took a swig of water. "I'm sure you've heard of the senior prank the year I graduated?"

"The goat on the football field?" she asked guardedly. "Anyone could do that."

"Not the goat on the field. Do you take me for an amateur?"

"Yes, because there's no way you could have pulled off the infamous one."

"What's so hard about putting a slip-and-slide covered in shaving cream in a hallway?" I asked.

"Not just the slip-and-slide, Mason," she said, getting excited. "It was set up between classes and no one saw it happen, and as soon as the janitor cleaned it up another one was set up in a different hallway. The principal had teachers walking the halls by the end of the day to keep it from happening again, but a third one still showed up—on the stage in the theater."

"The location was unfortunate," I conceded. "We were determined to set up the last one, but you're right, all the halls were too well guarded. Zack Batoully had a key, so we used the stage. We used shaving cream instead of water partly to avoid ruining the floors, but we didn't think about the wood floor on the stage."

"The school still talks about it."

I leaned back and grinned. "Scott and I came up with the whole plan."

"I don't believe you."

"Ask Mom when your slip-and-slide disappeared."

She grinned. "Well, I'll be damned. You *do* have some bad in you."

"Everyone has bad in them, Savannah. It's all in the execution and the intent."

Her smile faded and I worried I was about to lose her. "Some days I'm so pissed at Dad," I said.

She jerked up her head in surprise, but didn't speak.

"His job was to make sure that people's families are taken care of after they die and he screwed us over."

"How can you say that, Mason?" she asked in tears.

"Because it's true. He might not have meant to do it, but he did."

"But you love him. And he's dead. How can you be mad at him?" Her shell was cracking.

I leaned forward. "Just because he's dead doesn't mean I can't be mad at him. I'm furious." I stood and grabbed a rock, then threw it into the water. "You asshole!" I shouted. "You should have made sure we'd be okay!"

The stone hit the water with a thunk and Savannah watched me in horror.

I picked up another rock. "You said you'd be standing in the crowd when I graduated from Duke." I threw the rock as hard as I could. "You broke your promise!"

Savannah jumped up and grabbed my arm. "You can't be mad at him for that! He didn't want to die!"

"Maybe not, but he's still dead and I'm still pissed."

"If you love him, you can't be mad!"

"Why not?" I asked. "I love you and I'm so goddamned pissed at you right now."

Her eyes widened in shock.

"You are a beautiful, intelligent girl with a family that loves you more than you know and you are throwing your life away. So if I'm pissed at you, why can't I be pissed at him?"

"It's not right!" she shouted, tears streaming down her face. "We're not supposed to be mad at him."

I grabbed her shoulders. "Who says? Because you have every right to be mad." I dropped my hold and picked up a stone and placed it in her hand. "Tell him how you feel."

Horrified, she tried to shove it back at me. "No."

"You're mad at him, Savannah. It's written all over you. Tell. Him."

She half-heartedly threw the rock over the edge of the bluff. "You weren't supposed to leave me." Her voice broke. "I still need you, Daddy."

I put another stone in her hand.

She threw it harder this time. "You promised me that you'd fix the flat tire on my bike. *And it's still flat!*" she screamed.

I handed her another rock.

"You promised to teach me how to make your chocolate chip pancakes and you never did! *You liar*!"

She bent down and picked up her own rock and chucked it so forcefully, I worried she'd fall over. "You weren't supposed to leave me alone!" she wailed. "You're my daddy! You're supposed to walk me down the aisle and bounce my babies in your arms." She dropped to her knees. "You left me. How could you leave me?"

I dropped beside her and wrapped my arms around her as she sobbed. "You're not alone, Savannah. I'm not Dad, but I'll do all of those things for you and more."

"But he promised he would, and look how that turned out." She got to her feet. "He's dead."

I pulled her into a hug. "He meant it when he said it, just like I mean it now, but we both know I can't guarantee I won't die. Just like he couldn't."

She broke away from me. "Then what's the freaking point of any of this? To love someone just to lose them. *What's the freaking point?*"

I didn't answer her. I couldn't. My attempt to help her had only instigated a crisis of my own. What *was* the freaking point?

***

Savannah changed her group of friends and finished her senior year without much drama. Mom and I thought I'd gotten through to her somehow, and I had. Just not the way I'd planned. She'd taken my speech about finding sneakier friends to heart and was getting into more trouble than we realized at the time.

She tried going away to college, but came home halfway through the second semester of her freshman year after overdosing on Darvocet. And thus began a cycle of abuse and rehab, followed by a brief stint of productive behavior and then a relapse. Rinse and repeat.

But by the time she turned twenty-five, she seemed to have pulled herself together. She'd been clean for a year and was in her second year of law school. And then she met Joe Simmons and her world fell apart all over again.

She'd been seeing him for over a month when she called me and said she wanted me to meet her for lunch so she could introduce me to the guy she was dating.

"You're kidding?" I asked, rushing down the hall. I was an assistant DA in Little Rock by then, and I was on my way to court. "You've kept a guy around long enough to introduce him to me?"

"Says the man who hardly ever dates."

"I date." I laughed. "I went out with a paralegal just last week."

"And was there a second date?" she prompted.

"No. She was dull as dirt."

"You can't spend your life alone, Mason."

"Agreed. I can't see wasting my time on women who don't hold my interest either."

"But you have to get out there to find them! You're not going to find a wife stuck in your office."

"A *wife*? Who said anything about a wife? I'm just interested in sex."

My statement drew the horrified glance of an elderly woman in the hall.

"You can lie all you want, Mason Deveraux, but I know you. You're not a casual sex kind of guy."

"Unlike you," I teased.

"Not this time. Joe's a keeper."

"Joe, is it?"

"He has a sister. Maybe I'll set you two up."

"I think I'll pass. Imagine how well our relationship would fare when you dump Moe a few weeks from now."

"Joe. His name is Joe and I really like him." She paused, turning serious. "I think he's the one."

I stopped short outside the courtroom and moved away from the door. "Really? You've only known him for a month." Still, with all the men who'd traipsed in and out of Savannah's life, she'd never once made that statement.

"Sometimes you just know."

"Be careful with your heart, Savannah. Makes sure he deserves you."

"I think you're *too* careful with yours."

"Maybe I'm counting on finding *the one*. Just like you."

"So you'll meet him?" she asked excitedly.

"Of course. Name the time and the place."

We met for lunch a week later at a restaurant close to the courthouse. I tried to mask my surprise when I found out that Savannah's Joe was Joe Simmons. Based on his chilly reception, I presumed he'd heard of me too. In her excitement, Savannah failed to pick up on it.

Our conversation was stilted, both of us asking superficial questions and giving short responses. I studied him closely, watching for evidence that he loved her the way she obviously loved him. So far I'd seen no indication of that, which was making me angrier by the minute.

Savannah excused herself to go to the restroom and Joe and I stared at each other until I decided to be the better person. "It's apparent we don't care for each other."

Joe raised his eyebrows and gave me a cocky grin. "You think?"

"But we both care about Savannah. I love her and don't want to hurt her. I presume you want the same."

He leaned forward. "Look, Deveraux. I don't like you. You're a stuck-up prick who's fallen for his own PR."

"Excuse me?" I asked, as politely as I could manage. "PR?"

"You know, the educated rich white southern boy who goes to an elite school, then comes home and plays boy wonder in the courtroom. Well, all you really are is a self-righteous shithead who threw out two cases I worked my ass off to build."

I knew exactly which two cases he was talking about. "Maybe if you'd done it by the book, I would have had something to work with."

"If I'd done it by the book, none of that evidence would have come to light."

"Well we can't use it anyway," I said, "so what good did it do you?"

"I'm trying to get scum off the street."

"And I'm trying to make sure the defendants are really scum who deserve to be put away."

"Isn't that the defense attorney's job?" Joe asked.

Savannah returned to the table and stood by her chair. "Did I miss something?"

Joe got up and pulled her into a hug, then kissed her on the mouth. "I have to go. I'll call you later."

She held onto him as he started to pull away. "Is everything okay?"

He smiled down at her, finally showing her at least some of the adoration I'd been searching for. "Of course. I just got called in while you were gone. Can I still come over tonight? I can help you study for your test on torts."

She smiled, a dazzling smile I hadn't seen in years. In that moment, I decided that as long as Joe made her look like that, I could and would endure any shit he threw my way.

"He does know the torts you're studying aren't pastries, doesn't he?" I asked dryly as she sat down.

"Yes." She giggled. "He went to law school before he joined the state police."

"Did he now?"

Joe Simmons was full of all kinds of surprises.

Chapter Ten

Joe

Savannah had been pregnant. With my baby.

For some reason, knowing that had far more impact than the knowledge that Hilary was currently pregnant. Maybe it was because she'd been farther along. Or maybe it was because Deveraux had said the baby was a girl. No matter the reason, Savannah's baby was so much more real to me than the blob I'd seen on the ultrasound screen just that afternoon.

Mason leaned against the support post on my front porch, looking like he was about to murder me.

I sat down on one of the chairs on my porch, noticing that Mildred was peeking at us through the window across the street. I was surprised she hadn't called Henryetta's finest to check out the disturbance. The chief deputy sheriff dukin' it out with the assistant DA. That was sure to be big news even if Henryetta didn't have a gossip column in the *Henryetta Gazette*. Not that it needed one with Mildred butting in everyone's business.

Violet's porch light was on too, and it didn't surprise me a bit when she came marching over to investigate.

"*Mason?*" she asked when she noticed him by the post, then her gaze turned to me and she gasped. "What in God's name…" She spun around with her hands on her hips. "Punching Joe in Jasper's last week wasn't enough? You had to come over and beat him up at his own home? Does Rose know you're here?"

"Leave Rose out of this," Mason said, his voice pitched low.

"Leave her out of this? *Are you crazy?*" She stepped closer, jabbing her fingers into his chest. "Are you hurting my sister?"

"What?" Mason asked, obviously horrified. "No. Never."

"Then why did I see bruises on her arm?" Mason didn't answer, but Violet forged on, her voice taking on a menacing tone. "I swear to all that is holy, if I find out you've hurt one hair on her head, I will hunt you down and make you regret the day you ever laid eyes on her." She paused. "Have I made myself clear?"

"You're accusing the wrong person, Violet." Mason swiped at the blood trickling down his chin. "People seem to be lining up to hurt her, but I'm not one of them. From her perspective, you seem to be the first one in line."

"I've spent my entire life protecting Rose. Don't you even start with me." She turned to look at me. "Joe, do you want me to call the police?"

"Violet, in case you've forgotten," I said, looking up at her, "I *am* the police. Everything's fine here. Go on home."

She looked unconvinced, not that I blamed her. It was pretty damn clear we'd been in a fight.

I stood, my stomach aching from Mason's punch. "We're clearing the air. If we're both gonna live in this god-forsaken town, we have to learn to get along. Sometimes men get hot-headed and throw punches. It doesn't mean it's right, but this thing between Mason and me has been a long time coming. But we're done fighting—at least the physical part." I swung my hand toward Deveraux. "Right, Mason?"

"Yeah. That's right." His eyes hardened, negating his statement.

Not that I cared. Let him take a swing at me again if he wanted. I just needed Violet to get out of the way.

"Okay...if you're sure." She took baby steps toward my porch steps.

"Violet, go."

I waited until she reached her driveway. Then I lowered my voice and said, "I meant it when I said we need to clear the air."

"Shouldn't you be running back to Hilary in Little Rock?" Mason sneered. "Isn't that your MO? Leave her for a bit and use some poor woman before running to her? Savannah, Rose...and the others."

I started to protest, but Mildred was dead center in her window now, not even pretending to be subtle about her snooping. "Can we do this inside where we're not on display?"

He hesitated.

"Look, I don't know what Hilary's going to do, but I'm not going anywhere, Deveraux. I plan to stay in Fenton County. If you and I don't come to some kind of agreement, we're going to come to blows again. What if it's in front of Rose? Do you really want to do that to her a second time?"

"Fine."

I went through the front door, leaving Mason to follow me or not, not stopping until I reached the fridge and pulled out two beers. I handed him one as I sunk into the sofa, the sorry remnants of my dinner on the coffee table.

"Why are you here, Mason?" I asked as I popped the top off my beer. "Obviously, you've been saving that bombshell for a while. Why come tonight?"

"I'm trying to protect Rose."

I snorted. "More like trying to protect yourself." I took a long drag of my beer. "I bet Rose was horrified to hear that little nugget of info. Was that the deciding factor for her in choosing you?"

He stared at the unopened beer in his hand as if deciding whether he was going to stay long enough to justify opening it. "Rose doesn't know. No one does. Not even my mother."

That surprised me…and then it didn't. Mason Deveraux was a master at releasing information at just the right time during a trial. It made sense he'd do the same in real life. Tonight was proof enough of that.

"I've offered to give Rose the money to buy you out, but it's going to take a couple of weeks to get it. I want you to tell her you've changed your mind and you don't want to be a partner."

"No," I said, shaking my head and making my forehead throb. "Because I *do* want to be a partner."

"You and I both know you have no legal right to any say in the nursery."

I pressed the cool bottle to the growing knot on my brow. "And you and I both know she's going to give it to me anyway. Isn't that part of the reason you're here?"

Mason set his bottle on the side table with a bang. "You're a selfish son of a bitch, aren't you?"

I shrugged. There was no denying I had my own reasons for what I'd done, almost all of them selfish.

"Joe," his tone softened. "You've got your hands full with your ex-fiancée and her pregnancy. Please, just leave Rose alone. All she wants is a little peace. Her life has been nothing but chaos since her mother was killed. How much upheaval can one person take?"

"I know you find it hard to believe, Deveraux, but I love her. She's my everything."

"If you care so much about her, why aren't you doing anything to protect her from your father?"

I sucked in a breath, my anger simmering. He'd hated my father since he met him last year at a fundraiser I'd attended with Savannah.

I hated my father too, but I also knew what he was capable of doing to those who had stood up to him.

Whenever my father plotted to take someone down, he left a trail of devastation so tightly orchestrated even investigators using a microscope could never tie it back to him. He wielded his power on the highest of political officials as well as the lowliest members of the house staff. J.R. Simmons was a man of extremes. He was either your best friend or your worst enemy. There was no middle ground. And no one wanted to be in the path of his wrath.

When I was eight, I eavesdropped on my father as he berated an employee for losing money on an investment. I'd watched in horror and fascination as the man cried and pleaded for my father's mercy. But I learned that day my father didn't believe in mercy. "I will ruin you," he said, and then he fired the man and sent him out the door. Within seconds of the employee leaving, my father called the bank and convinced them to find a way to foreclose on the man's home.

My father didn't bat an eye before destroying anyone who got in his way. But if I toed the line, there was nothing to worry about.

I shook my head. "As long as I'm not running for office, she's fine."

Mason stood. "Are you even listening to what you're saying? Leaving that threat hanging over her head is like playing Russian roulette. You're seriously going to do that?"

I jumped to my feet. "What the hell do you want me to do, Deveraux? My hands are tied!"

His eyes hardened. "You claim to love her—prove it. I'm going to stop him. If you care anything about her, help me do it."

"*What?* You're going to take on my father? Are you crazy? Do you have the slightest idea of what he's capable of?"

Mason's expression softened and his eyes pleaded with me. "I know you don't want to hear this, but I love her too. It makes me crazy to think about her being sent to prison—even for a day—because of your father's lies. I'd give up everything and drag her halfway around the world to protect her from your father, but she'd never agree to leave her family and friends."

"Save the drama for the courtroom, Deveraux. I would never let that happen."

"How could you stop it?"

I didn't answer. I didn't *have* an answer. Anyone who tried to defy him was crushed.

"Joe, something bad is about to happen. I can feel it. Your father's going to use his weapon, and I need to be prepared to stop him." He paused. "Help me."

"No. You're crazy."

"Then I'll do it without you." He turned and headed for the door.

"Leave it alone, Mason," I called after him. "If my father even catches wind that you're up to something, he'll blow it all to kingdom come. That will hurt her even worse."

"Not if I get to him first."

Chapter Eleven

Rose

I knew something was wrong even before Mason glanced at his phone after dinner, then said he was going into the office. But I watched him walk out the door certain there was nothing I could do about it. I also suspected it had something to do with Joe, but I wasn't sure what to do about that either. So I wasn't surprised when Violet called me about thirty minutes later.

"Did you know Mason's at Joe's house right now?"

My stomach twisted in knots. "No."

"They were out on his front porch causing a commotion, so I went over to check it out. Both of their faces were bleeding, so I think they got into some kind of a scuffle."

"Bad?" I forced out.

"No. Mason's lip and Joe's eyebrow. And they weren't fightin' when I got over there. They weren't saying *anything*. They acted like they were waiting for me to leave."

"Is Mason still there?"

"Yeah. Joe said he and Mason were done hitting each other, but they had some things to work out. Then they disappeared into Joe's house."

"Do you hear them shoutin'?"

"No, but Miss Mildred's about to fall out her window screen trying to figure out what's goin' on." She paused. "Oh, wait. Mason's leaving now. You know, for a guy with a busted leg, he's sure getting around."

"Yeah…" My stomach was a mess with nerves.

"Rose, I'm really scared for you."

"*Why?*" What did she know that I didn't?

"This is twice in one week that Mason has been part of a physical fight."

"Both times with Joe," I added. "He provokes him."

"The first time Joe never lifted a finger. We were both witnesses."

"For all we know Joe threw the first punch this time," I said.

"Rose," Violet said slowly, as though she was explaining something to Mikey. "Mason showed up on Joe's doorstep. He instigated this." She hesitated. "And I know he put those bruises on your arm. Deny it."

I paused. What could I say? I didn't want to lie to her. "He had a nightmare and grabbed me. He didn't mean to hurt me and was horrified when he realized what had happened." Oh, Lord. What had I done? Why had I admitted that to Violet of all people? "You can't tell Joe."

"Rose, Joe is a deputy sheriff now and you live outside of city limits. The sheriff is who you call for domestic violence cases."

"Good heavens, Violet! Just let it go! I told you it was an accident."

"I want you to promise me something." She sounded worried and serious. "If Mason ever threatens you or he hurts you, I want you to call Joe."

"Not you?" I asked in a snotty tone. How dare she think so badly of Mason!

"No. I might not be able to help you. But Joe can. Promise me."

Her request was utterly ridiculous, but I could hear tears in her voice, and I wanted to ease her mind. "Okay. I promise."

"Thank you. I know you have a hard time believing it, but I really do love you. I've just done a bad job of showing it lately."

"I love you too."

"I'm gonna try to be a better sister. I don't want to lose you."

"You're stuck with me as a sister for life. We'll talk more about the business next week."

I hung up and helped Maeve finish cleaning up the kitchen.

"My real estate agent called and asked me to meet him at the house tomorrow morning before I head back to Little Rock," she said as she dried the crock pot lid. "I thought you might like to come see it."

"I'd love to. I'm so excited that you're moving to Henryetta."

"Me too." She beamed at me. "I'm supposed to meet the Realtor at eleven to go over some things from the inspection, but if you join me there at around eleven-fifteen, I'll show you around. It's tiny, so it won't take long."

"It sounds wonderful. And I want to help you get moved and settled."

Muffy started whining, then released a cloud of poisonous gas. "Goodness, Muffy," I choked out, waving my hand in front of my face as Maeve started coughing. "I've tried eight different dog foods and I swear your stench is getting worse." I tossed my dish towel onto the counter and headed for the front door. "Let's go outside, Muff, although I hope we don't kill off any plant life. You're like a mini-Chernobyl."

I grabbed my coat as Muffy ran past me through the door and out to the yard. I sat on the front steps and watched her make a nasty pile by a dead bush at the corner of the house. She wasn't in a hurry to go in and neither was I since I was so nervous about what Mason had been up to so I watched her romp around. Ten minutes later, Mason's headlights appeared in the driveway. He pulled the car to a stop in front of the old farmhouse and got out, his leg dragging as he walked toward the porch.

He stopped in front of me, resignation on his face. "Violet called you."

I nodded, then bolted off the step and threw myself at him, wrapping my arms around his neck.

His back was tense, but as soon as he realized I wasn't going to berate him, he pulled me tight against him and sighed, rustling the hair by my ear.

"What happened?"

"I think we've reached a truce of sorts."

I pulled back to look up at his face. I could see his busted lip even in the dim porch light. "What does that mean?"

"For the moment, it means we probably won't feel like beating the crap out of each other whenever we're in the same room."

"That's a start, I guess."

"True enough." He grinned, then winced at the way it jarred his injured lip.

"I'm glad to hear that you two aren't going to be brawling in public places." I rubbed my thumb under his lip. "You have such a handsome face and I hate to see it messed up. Not to mention it gets in the way of me kissing you." I stretched up and placed a gentle kiss on the opposite corner of his mouth.

"You're not mad?"

"That you went to see Joe? No. I'm not surprised you did after finding out about his investment."

He sighed, sounding weary. "You're worth every bit of conflict I have to endure with Joe Simmons."

"Anything I need to know about from your meeting other than that you both got hit?"

He paused. "He's dead-set on being a partner even though he knows he has no legal claim to your business. He refused to let me buy him out."

I started to protest, but he stopped me. "I had to try, Rose. I'm sorry."

"I know." It surprised me that he'd tried to buy out Joe after promising to leave the matter up to my judgment. But he'd already confessed how worried he was about losing me, so I couldn't be too mad. It was actually encouraging to know that Mason, who always did what was right, had a few flaws. And of course, while he'd told what amounted to a white lie, I'd helped crown the new crime king of Fenton County. "It's okay."

"I want to reiterate that you don't have to let him have any say, but I know you...and you will. But I'm begging you to please ask me if you need any more help."

"I *do* want your help—I already told you I do—and you'll probably get sick to death of me pestering you for your opinion. I have a lot of decisions to make, and I'm feeling a bit overwhelmed."

He grinned, getting a mischievous look in his eye. "If you're gonna kill me by overwhelming me, I'd rather you do it in our bed."

I laughed. "I'd rather not kill you at all, but that does sound like a promising challenge."

He tugged me closer and whispered in my ear, his voice husky, "Then we *definitely* need to go upstairs."

Later as I lay in Mason's arms after he'd gone to sleep, I was certain not telling him about the Lady in Black was the right thing to do.

Perhaps it was for the best. I should keep her in the closet, stuffed into the back where she belonged.

Chapter Twelve

Joe

After several days of sleepless nights spent thinking about Rose, and the handful of occasions we'd spent time together in the house where I now lived alone, I knew I couldn't stay there. But that night, I tossed and turned for a different reason—my sleep was haunted with memories of Savannah.

It would have been easy to throw all the blame of our breakup on Hilary, but I realized I had to take responsibility for it too. Just like I had to take responsibility for Savannah's death. And the baby's. I hadn't loved Savannah, not like I loved Rose, but I'd cared about her. I owed her something. The fact that she was dead and I couldn't do one damn thing to help her was obvious, but the desire to atone for my sins kept me awake.

I had Saturday off. I considered making arrangements to clean up the nursery, but I wanted to talk to Rose first. She would hopefully be more receptive now that she'd had the chance to cool down, but if she was dead set against it, I'd back off, despite what I'd led Mason to believe. Still, I wasn't about to tell her that and give her an easy out. I really did want to be part of the business. I'd play it by ear.

Instead, I called a real estate agent and asked her to line up a list of houses for sale both in Henryetta city limits and outside. She called back half an hour later with a short list and gave me the first address, telling me to meet her there at eleven.

I pulled up in front of a house that looked like a cottage, surprised to see two other cars out front. As I walked up to the door, I saw that it was cracked open and heard voices inside.

I pushed my way inside and looked around. The house was cute—matching the cottage exterior. Most of the furnishings had been removed. All I could see was a beat-up arm chair by the fireplace with a small table and lamp—most likely a pathetic attempt to stage the house—and a small kitchen table with four chairs.

A man stood next to the brick fireplace, holding a stack of papers. He was talking to an older woman who stood next to him. "The report's not bad," he said. "Just a bunch of little things you'd expect to find in a house this age. But you got it for a steal, so I'm not sure how many of the repairs the owners will agree to make. You'll probably have to arrange to fix them on your own. Perhaps your son?"

A woman laughed. "My son is capable of many things, but home repair doesn't fall on that list."

The man turned and gave me a quizzical look.

I flashed him a smile. "I was told to meet my Realtor here at eleven, but it looks like this house already has an offer on it. Sorry to interrupt."

"You're the new sheriff deputy, aren't you?" he asked, moving a few steps closer. "Glad to have you in town. My name's Artie Mussels." He looked back over his shoulder. "And this is the assistant D.A.'s mother, Maeve Deveraux."

I felt like I'd been punched in the gut, only the sensation was ten times worse than when this woman's son had punched me the night before.

She smiled, the expression lighting up her face, and I was blown away by how much she resembled Savannah. "Nice to meet you," she said. "I suspect you might end up working with my son."

I nodded, feeling like I was about to puke. "Yes, ma'am. We already have worked together."

"Oh?" she asked. "You know Mason?"

I stood in the threshold, seriously contemplating turning around and getting the hell out of there, but it was time to face up to my past—every last bit of it—and this seemed like a monumental place to start. I took several hesitant steps closer to her. "Yes, ma'am. I do." I swallowed. "And I knew your daughter. Savannah."

Confusion wrinkled her forehead. "How…"

"Mrs. Deveraux…I used to live in Little Rock. My name's Joe Simmons."

Her eyes flew open and she took a step backward.

"Maeve? Are you okay?" Artie asked as he rushed forward to grab her elbow.

I moved toward her out of instinct and started to reach for her, then pulled back, unsure if she wanted the man responsible for her daughter's death to touch her.

She took a breath and patted the Realtor's hand. "Thank you, Artie. I'm just a little surprised. It's such a small world. Joe dated my daughter."

"Oh."

"Artie, could you give us a moment?" I asked. "Mrs. Deveraux and I need to catch up on a few things."

He glanced at Savannah's mother; she nodded and gave him a gentle smile.

"I'll just be outside making a few calls," he said, heading for the door.

"And if my agent shows up," I called after him, "can you tell her I'll be out in a moment?"

"Sure thing," Artie mumbled, already looking at his phone.

"Would you like to sit?" I asked, motioning toward the kitchen table in the dining room. "It might make this easier. For both of us."

She nodded and pulled out a chair. I resisted the urge to help her with it—old habits die hard—but I was already pressing my luck. I sat on the opposite side from her, folding my hands on the table.

We sat in silence for several seconds before I cleared my throat. "First of all...I'd like to say how profoundly sorry I am." My voice broke and I blinked to ease the burning in my eyes. "I'm sure you hate me, and I understand why you would."

Her chin quivered and she wiped her fingertips under her right eye. "I don't hate you, Joe."

I studied her, wondering if she was telling the truth. "How can you not hate me? Your daughter died because of me."

"She died because some man with a mental illness became fixated on her and stabbed her to death." Her voice broke and she bit her upper lip. "Everyone is so eager to take the blame for her death—you, Mason, the police—I wish you all would just let it go and blame the person who is truly responsible. Michael Cartwright. Her murderer."

Let it go? I'd soaked myself in the guilt of my actions for months. It was part of who I was now. I wasn't sure I was capable of letting it go.

She forced a smile through her tears. "No, I don't hate you, Joe. It's the truth, even if you find it hard to believe. I should have reached out to you after Savannah's death, but…I didn't. I wanted to respect your privacy. I realize now that it was wrong."

My eyes widened in shock. "Why would you have reached out to *me*? It should have been the other way around, but I was a coward. I couldn't even go to her funeral."

She studied me for a moment. "But you *were* there."

I froze.

"You weren't at the gravesite—which was probably a good thing because Mason might have strangled you—but I saw you a ways away, behind a tree. Watching. I knew it was you." She wiped her cheek again. "And I said a prayer for you."

"*Me?*"

She chuckled. "Yes, you. I prayed that you would find the peace and strength to move forward from this tragedy." She paused. "Have you, Joe?"

My shoulders shook as I tried to hold back tears. "I thought I had. And then I lost her." I stared into Mrs. Deveraux's eyes. "To your son."

She nodded. "Rose."

"I love her. It doesn't feel right telling you that given the circumstances, but I do."

"I know the three of you are caught in quite a dilemma." She looked down at the table and rubbed her thumb over a scratch in the wood. "I'd like to give you a piece of advice, Joe. Take it or leave it, considering the source."

"Okay…"

She looked up at me, her soft eyes holding mine. "You thought you had found your peace and strength in Rose. And I can see why you're so taken with her. But I think you need to find your peace and strength in *yourself*. If you find it in someone else, that person will be destined to disappoint you and let you down. But if you find it in yourself, you will be a richer person, and your relationships will be richer for it."

"You're just telling me that because she's with Mason."

Her eyes hardened slightly. "I gave Mason that same piece of advice this past summer." She stood. "Trust me,

Joe. I learned it the hard way when my husband died. You want the woman you love to complement you, not be the air you breathe. Not a day goes by without me wishing I'd given Savannah that same advice."

She started for the door.

"If I'd known about the b—" I stopped, realizing what I was about to say.

She froze and turned to face me. "The baby?"

I stood and held onto the back of the chair. "You know?"

"Of course I know," she sighed. "Mason thinks he's protecting me by not telling me what he found out in the autopsy report, but of course I know. I'm Savannah's mother. *She* told me."

"Why didn't she tell *me?*"

"Because she finally realized that she couldn't make you love her. She couldn't make you want to be with her. She loved you, but she wanted you to be with her because it was your choice. Not because you felt it was your duty."

"I'm sorry I couldn't be…that for her."

"So was she." Mrs. Deveraux walked out the front door.

I stood next to the chair, trying to deal with what had just happened. Too many blows were hitting me all at once.

I heard voices outside the door. I realized I needed to pull myself together and leave, but then the door opened and Rose stood in the threshold.

"Joe?" She sounded worried as she crossed the room. When she reached me, she pulled me close for a hug. "Are you okay?"

For one brief moment, I thought she had chosen me. The disappointment that followed was suffocating. "Yeah," I choked out.

"Maeve told me about your conversation—not the details—just that you suggested you two should talk." She looked up at me. "I'm so proud of you."

"I'm not sure I'm worthy of your pride. Nothing I can do now will ever change the past."

"But it can change your future."

"Savannah doesn't have a future." Our baby didn't have a future either. I held back a sob.

"If she loved you, and I'm certain she did, she would want you to have a happy future."

I didn't answer, fighting back my tears.

Rose grabbed my arm, and the expression she always got when she was really determined about something washed over her face. I had to stop myself from kissing her.

"But if you want to make Savannah proud of you, you need stop going back to Hilary every time something bad happens. She's like a cancer, Joe, and she's slowly killing you, bit by bit."

"I know. But she's pregnant. With my baby."

"You're sure it's yours?"

"Yes."

"Then you'll be the best father that baby could ever hope for, because with her as mother, that baby's gonna need you. But not together with Hilary. Separate."

"I don't know if I can do this alone."

Her shoulders lifted. "You won't be alone. You'll have plenty of friends around you to help. Especially if you stay in Fenton County."

"And what about you?"

Her face softened. "I'll always be your friend, Joe. If you'll let me."

I nodded.

"We'll discuss the business next week." Her eyes narrowed. "But I'm telling you right now—Bruce Wayne is going to be my partner too so you best get over it real quick or your tenure with the Gardner Sisters Nursery is gonna be the shortest tenure in history."

I chuckled. God, she was a spitfire. "I can live with that."

"Okay." She smiled and gave an involuntary shake. "Then this might actually work out after all."

I watched her walk out the door and pulled out my phone. "Deveraux? What you said about going after my father…I'm in."

***

Thirty-Three and a Half Shenanigans
November 4, 2014.

About the Author

Denise Grover Swank was born in Kansas City, Missouri and lived in the area until she was nineteen. Then she became a nomadic gypsy, living in five cities, four states and ten houses over the course of ten years before she moved back to her roots. She speaks English and smattering of Spanish and Chinese which she learned through an intensive Nick Jr. immersion period. Her hobbies include witty Facebook comments (in own her mind) and dancing in her kitchen with her children. (Quite badly if you believe her offspring.) Hidden talents include the gift of justification and the ability to drink massive amounts of caffeine and still fall asleep within two minutes. Her lack of the sense of smell allows her to perform many unspeakable tasks. She has six children and hasn't lost her sanity. Or so she leads you to believe.

36930204R00092